A Novella

LIGHTWAVES

DAVID EDGAR GRINNELL

QUILLKEEPERS PRESS

Cover design, image, & title image licensed through Shutterstock; altered and formatted by Quillkeepers Press
Editing by Stephanie Lamb and Amber Romero
Formatting by Quillkeepers Press

Printed in the United States of America

Quillkeepers Press
P.O. Box 10236
Casa Grande, Arizona 85130
https://www.quillkeeperspress.com

https://davidpg17.wixsite.com/davidpgbooks

Cataloging-in-publication data is on file with the Library of Congress

*"To forget the dead would be akin to killing them a second time." -
Elie Wiesel*

Table of Contents

CHAPTER ONE

April 16, 2012

I swear I have the worst luck on this entire planet! I'm a scrawny, helpless squirrel trying to find his nut to survive the frigid winter! I can't seem to find my nut, and I'm not saying I like to go outside to search for acorns, but my problem is life. I mean, life has some great moments but seriously…. When do I get my piece of cheese? I'm a lab mouse going around in circles and dead ends in a maze. Honestly, I believe I would probably have better luck finding a donkey eating the headrest of my car than life turning around in my favor, for once. I'm from horse country, the state of Kentucky. I moved out to Washington, DC, for a job working at a history museum. Of course, I used to work there…. My clumsy self accidentally crashed into an exhibit while trying to get my car keys.

I was swirling them around my finger while looking at the World War II airplane exhibit. I was on my fifteen-minute break. I didn't pay

attention while swirling the keys around, and that's when it happened....
My keys suddenly fling off my finger and straight into the cockpit of a
Spitfire II.

"Dang it," I mutter quietly, looking around, hoping that neither my
boss nor any other employees will see what I am about to do.

I climb over the cordon towards the Spitfire II, and I jump to reach
into the cockpit to get my keys that are inside. I struggle to jump up as I
can't get myself in the cockpit due to its height. It's slightly hanging
above the ground. Finally, with one powerful jump, I got onto the Spitfire
with my hands inside the cockpit. I pull myself up. Suddenly, I hear a
loud creaking sound.

A few moments later, the plane crashes down and makes a loud
ruckus. My boss hears the loud noise, rushes into the room, and sees me
in the cockpit with just my legs in the air. The wings on the aircraft are
detached, but they loosely dangle. Talk about broken wings, and that's
all she wrote – I am shown the door after getting out of the plane. My
boss was always a stuck-up hippo since he hired me and didn't have the
patience or tolerance for people.

Once getting fired, I amble to my car parked on the side of the street,
but when I get there, I observe it getting towed away. The tow truck
driver shows me the paper explaining why it's getting taken away, it's
not facing the right direction, and the car is incorrectly parked. I grip and
crumble the paper while lifting my head. I stare at the sky, blaming

myself; I should pay more attention when running late to work. I listen; my car tows away. Tiny raindrops hit my face, and I glare straight forward, reaching into my pockets. I don't have any cash on me for a taxicab.... I must walk all the way to my small apartment. By the time I reach halfway to my apartment, the rain downpours upon me.

I trudge into my apartment, drenched with water. It drips down my hair and coat. I drop my jacket off, it falls on the back of the kitchen chair, and I grab a can of soda while drying my hair with a paper towel. I sip the soda and shuffle towards my computer desk, turning it on. I wait a while for my computer to start and open a typing application. In my spare time, I love to write and type stories, mostly about anything that comes to mind. I've been writing historical fiction lately because I love history so much. Also, there's nothing like getting lost in writing after a stressful day.

My computer opens research on World War II. I hope an idea will pop into my head to write a good book; however, after an hour or so, no idea comes to mind. I glare towards my window. The rain still pounds, my eyes shift back to my computer, and it's late. So, I figure I should hit the sack and have a walk tomorrow around DC to see if any other museums are interested in hiring me.

The next day, I have a small breakfast – sausage biscuits from the freezer and head out the door to follow my plan. I spend most of the morning going from museum to museum, filling out job applications.

Soon, noon approaches, and I decide to visit one more museum; the Holocaust Museum. I am at the main entrance and read the description on the wall outside:

"Out of our memory... of the Holocaust we must forge an unshakable oath with all civilized people that never again will the world stand silent. Never again will the world... Fail to act in time to prevent this terrible crime of genocide... We must harness the outrage of our own memories to stamp out oppression wherever it exists. We must understand that human rights and human dignity are indivisible."

Curiosity grips my heart; I am intrigued by the scripture and mooch inside. As I enter, I am handed a card of a person who was murdered in the Holocaust. Further inside, I go into a small confined-spaced elevator with several other people. It's rather uncomfortable as the tour guide briefs upon a few things about the Holocaust. The elevators stop on a floor that shows the chronological history of the Holocaust. It starts with the Nazis rising to power. Several TV screens display images from the Holocaust, and several artifacts are also on display.

I learn about Aryan ideology, ghettos, and the Final Solution. I toddle on the self-guided tour for I don't know how many hours I spend looking around. A heavy weight in my heart seethes, for the presence within the tour is haunting. I come across one of the train cabs where the trains haul all the Jews to the camps. I plod inside the empty train cab, look around, then close my eyes, trying to imagine how overcrowded it was within the cab. Closing my eyes, I hear the train clicking along the tracks, the presence of cramped people within the cab silently weeping, and finally, the screeching halt of the train with its whistle blowing and arriving at the death and labor camps.

Reopening my eyes, I trudge out of the train cab on the other side and continue the self-guided tour. Suddenly, my foot lightly steps onto something small and round. I halt myself from stepping on the object and look at what it is. It's some kind of gold ring; I glance and pick it up from the ground to take a closer look.

Studying the gold ring in my hand, I discover an inscription inside the band:

"Michael Luke Adelman," I say to myself, seeing it barely engraved.

The ring is rather worn, and I conclude that this ring must be a wedding ring. Therefore, it must belong to the man whose name is engraved on this ring.

My head swivels around to see if the person that dropped this ring is about, but nobody is in sight. I roam onward through the tour, hoping to run into the person to whom this ring belonged. I ask around, talking to random people, asking if this ring is theirs, but it belongs to nobody. Finally, I finish the tour and end up in the hall of remembrance. It's the place within the museum where people would honor and pray in memory of those who lived and died during the Holocaust. I squeeze the ring in my hand, glance down at it, and move it around.

"I can't just leave it here," I speak to myself as I rush to the front desk and ask an employee.

"Excuse me; someone has misplaced this ring."

The employee's eyes focus on the computer, typing away.

"Oh, just drop it in the plastic tub...."

My eyes observe the tub full of random items, and her fingers rapidly click against the keys. Her voice replays in my head, *"Oh, just drop it in the plastic tub...."* Her voice was apathetic. In contemplation, my mind races, and not once has she looked at me or this ring. This employee isn't going to honor this ring.... Look at all these lost items! I grip the ring in my hand. I must keep the ring, take good care of it, and hope that I can find the owner of this ring. I want to give it back. I groan; the woman's fingers continue to drum against the keyboard, and I exit the building in disgust.

The lukewarm breeze plays upon my cheeks as I stump back to my apartment, thinking about this ring. I study it again as there's something else engraved on the inside. My eyes squint. I can't see it clearly, so I dig out the magnifying glass to look closer. There are three numbers carved: "20/9/42," and after the number forty-two, there is the Star of David. Whoever owns this ring is Jewish.

After studying the ring, I placed it inside a small box and set it on my nightstand. My stomach rumbles – I need to get something to eat. I chow down on ramen noodles and think about the next plan of action.

Searching for a job today was somewhat successful.... My eyes catch a glimpse of my fridge; I left it open.

"I need to hit the grocery store tomorrow. Perhaps I can apply at the grocery store to see if my luck will change. I'm desperate...."

David Edgar Grinnell

CHAPTER TWO

Spring 1941

"Michael, are you going to ask her yet?" whispers Michael's friend Ben in class. Michael turns around from his desk at Ben and shifts back to the front of the classroom. The students wait for the teacher to arrive. "I'm telling you, Michael, you should just go and ask her out on a date," adds Ben.

Soon, the teacher arrives in the class to begin the day, "I'm sorry, students, for keeping you waiting," says the teacher setting her bag and coat at her desk.

The teacher grips the chalk, writing down the assignment for her students on the chalkboard. When she is halfway done writing the agenda on the board, she breaks down weeping but trying to fight off her tears. She drops the chalk in her hand and leans her head against the chalkboard. There is a moment of silence as all her students wonder what is wrong.

The teacher takes a moment to compose herself; she shifts to the class, "They came and took my husband away last night. I arrived home after grading the class's test papers at the school. When I came home, he was gone – everything in the house left broken.... They took him away...." shallows the teacher, still trying to hold herself together. Soon, she bellows and, in moments, croaks, "Class dismissed early; I'm sorry, children," she scuttles out of the classroom. All the students in the class hear the teacher's weeping inside the halls, and her footsteps lollop in echoes, becoming fainter.

Everyone sits in silence until Emily Dembitz, Michael's crush, storms out of the classroom crying. Ben encourages Michael to go after her and encourages him to talk to her. A few seconds pass as Michael follows out of the classroom to speak with Emily. He catches a glimpse of Emily's figure pushing out the main school doors, sobbing. She sits outside on the steps with her head on her lap. Michael follows her, stands outside for a moment, and sits next to her on the steps. He doesn't say anything for a moment until he finally speaks her name, "Emily...."

"Another Jewish family taken away by the SS Police... Now, Mrs. Brodowski is alone," says Emily.

"You have to stay strong, Emily," replies Michael.

"Michael, I don't know how much longer I can stand this...we're not allowed to ride bicycles, go to public schools, or go to regular stores because we're Jews," mewls Emily glancing down at the Star of David on her school blouse. Michael touches Emily's hand, trying to comfort her.

"I'm scared, Michael.... I don't want to see my parents go being separated from them like how our teacher Mrs. Brodowski's husband, was. Do you think it's true what people are saying about the death camps? Do you think my parents and I will be taken away?" she asks, holding Michael's hand tightly.

"Honestly, I don't have an answer for that, Emily. All I know is that things aren't going to get better for us, but we must fight through this, pray, and hope for the best; we can't give up," replies Michael.

"Aren't you afraid, Michael?" cries Emily looking at him.

"Yes, of course, I'm afraid, but like I said, we must be strong. I wish I didn't have to wear this star on my clothes so I wouldn't be pushed around so much; I could kill those German Nazis myself!" yowls Michael, his hand over the Jewish star on his coat.

"But that's the Magen David..." putters Emily.

"Yes, I know, and even if I ripped this off my shirt, I would be shot and killed for it," replies Michael.

"You'd never do that, would you?" scrunches Emily with concern.

"No, of course not!" whirrs Michael highly.

"Good, because you mean too much to me to be killed!" says Emily.

Michael smiles, "Really?"

Emily's eyes are warm, "Yes, you mean an awful lot to me, and we've been friends since I can remember. You've always been there for me."

Michael stares into Emily's eyes, "I'll always be there for you, Emily, for better or worse, no matter what happens!"

Emily takes a moment as her eyes lock with Michael's. "Do you promise me?" she demands, sinking her lips.

"Yes, I promise with all my heart, you'll always have a place in my heart to keep you safe, a place in my heart you can always call home no matter where you are," replies Michael.

Emily scoots over to Michael, kisses him on the cheek, and hugs him tightly. She holds onto him, "My knight in shining armor," says Emily softly, still holding Michael close.

Michael wraps his arms around Emily and holds her close to him. It is the only place where he always keeps her close, his heart.

Later that night, Michael is at his house with his parents doing his homework in the dining room. His parents are in the parlor listening to the radio until the sound of sirens begins wailing from outside. Then, Michael's father switches off the radio and hears the sirens growing louder, and their sound blare from down the street.

"They're coming; the Gestapo!" shouts Michael's father. Michael's heart sinks after hearing his father's words. He observes his father and mother rushing toward him.

Michael's father quickly grabs his son and pulls him off the chair, "Go, son, leave and go out the back!" He yells. Michael's father pushes him toward the backdoor of the house.

"Dad, I can't leave you and mom behind!" shouts Michael as he starts to tear up.

"Son, I said get out of here! Don't worry about your mother and me. It's more important to us that you go somewhere safe."

Michael's father rushes over to a case inside the dining room cabinet. Inside is his World War I German Luger pistol. Tears stream from Michael's eyes as his mother gives him a hug and a kiss on the forehead.

"Go!" says Michael's mother.

"I love you, mom...." mutters Michael's brittle voice.

Michael's father clicks back the German luger, ready to fire as the gray trucks are near the door with the sound of the engines running.

They hear several footsteps. The footsteps storm up to the front door, and fists pound on it, "erschließen, erschließen," one of the Germans shouts.

"Go now!" screams Michael's mother to him.

Michael looks at both of his parents for a moment, then runs off to the backdoor escaping.

When Michael makes it outside to his backyard, he listens to the front door of his house smashed down. A gunshot echoes. Michael's body jolts, his eyes fixate back on his home, and for a moment, he wonders what is happening. Another gunshot echoes. Michael bolts cutting through backyards and away from the house. He hears his mother crying and screaming at the top of her lungs.

Michael makes it to the end of the street. Looking back at the gray vehicles from far away, he sees his mother dragged, tossed into a truck, and two Nazi soldiers carrying out his father's body. The two soldiers heave the body and leave it on the street. They get inside the truck and drive away.

The Nazis shift the truck in reverse as they drive out onto the street. When they place the vehicle in reverse, Michael's father's lifeless body crackles under the tires. The driver switches the vehicle to drive, and the tires crush over the body again. Michael stands still, watching all before him with the gray trucks speeding away in the distance.

CHAPTER THREE

April 18, 2012

So, it's just another day for me…. Ugh, filling out a lengthy job application at one of the food stores in DC. I'd have better luck eating popcorn, watching the paint dry on a wall, and drooling on myself while growing facial hair. So far, no such luck getting a job, but I walk to the bank to get some cash and go back to the store so I can buy some food. I am running low on a few items at home. I hate taking money out of my account, but I must put food on my table, not unless; I grab a BB gun and shoot a squirrel in broad daylight.

Eh, that probably wouldn't work out too well…. I can see myself getting chased by the scrawny little guy after pissing him off by shooting a BB gun at him. Oh well, I must do what's necessary: go to the store. As I head down an aisle, I observe an employee unloading canned goods and stocking them on the shelves. I'm distracted and looking in the other direction until suddenly, I hear a loud crash.

I turn and see the employee's fresh goods on his cart scattered all over the floor. Cans roll everywhere as I rush over to help him.

"Oh, thank you, sir," replies the employee kindly.

"Not a problem," I say to him, picking up cans. As I'm helping the clerk, I am unaware of what's behind me as I go backward on my quest for other cans and stumble on a rouge can behind me on the floor.

Stumbling, I lose my balance and find myself crashing into the shelves behind me. The entire display plummets down, and a young woman screams from the aisle next to the shelf that crashes down.

"Dang it; my clumsy-self did it again!" I exclaim, hobbling over to where the young woman is.

"Are you alright, ma'am?" I roar, removing all the cans on top of her while helping her up.

"Yes, I'm fine," she answers, standing on her feet. The young woman has long, dark hair and deep, brown eyes as she smiles at me.

A few seconds pass, and she turns frantic, "Oh, my necklace!" she shouts, clutching her hand between her neck and chest. She panics, looking for it in all the cans of rubble, and I alongside assist her.

A few moments later, I find the necklace and fish it out of the rubble. When I have it in my hand, the necklace's pendant has six tiny diamonds on each corner of the Jewish star: the Star of David.

"Is this yours?" I inquired to her as she was still looking.

"Oh yes, it is!" she shouts with relief as I give it to her.

She places it around her neck, and I introduce myself to her. "I'm Charlie Campel," I take her hand as we both rise from the floor.

She smiles at me, "Luna Braun," the young woman states.

Soon, the employee I tried to help returns with the manager. He is boiling with rage and sees the entire shelf knocked down with all the canned goods all over the floor.

"If you can…. Please leave!" the manager asks as nicely as he can, with the rage still building up.

Luna and I purchase the items in our baskets and exit the store together.

"That was crazy. I'm so clumsy!" I add, walking next to her as we enter the parking lot.

Luna smiles with a chuckle, "It's alright, it's over now. Are you always that clumsy?" she asks.

"You have no idea," I say as I help her put groceries in her car.

Once the groceries are safely loaded, she turns and says, "Thanks for helping me, packing my groceries in the car, and most importantly, finding my necklace."

I smile at her, "You're welcome; it was nice meeting you!"

"Likewise," she adds, and I nod, beginning to amble out to the parking lot.

I am halfway out until Luna shouts out to me.

"Charlie, where are you going? Don't you have a car?" she pings out to me.

I stop from leaving as I turn around, shaking my head.

"Would you like a lift?" she gestures at me.

"Oh yes, thank you!" I glee back, running to Luna's car.

Suddenly, as I am lightly running, the grocery bags I'm carrying pop open. All my goods scatter across the ground. I halt as I stand there for a moment, heavily sighing, and slump my head down with the now empty bags still in my hands. They are opened from the bottom.

I glance up a bit and catch a glimpse of Luna shrouding her hand over her face. She laughs at what she is witnessing while she helps me gather my scattered groceries in the parking lot.

Once everything is accounted for, we load my groceries into her car. As we finish, Luna laughs. I see her head dipped down and her lips tighten. I get in the passenger side. My mouth creases into a grin. I fidget in the seat as my eyes wander to her. Luna's lips sink and smudge together. She closes her door and plops her elbow on the door's armrest. Luna's eyes anchor, and we stare.

"I'm sorry," she mutters, trying to control her laughter.

"It's alright; I laugh at myself a lot of times...." I joke with a smile as I laugh with her.

Luna drives me home to my small apartment and helps me with my groceries. She stores some of them inside my condensed kitchen cabinets.

We catch glimpses of each other as we finish up. My limbs ache with every exchange of our tender gazes, and Luna bites her lip as she stands by my apartment door. "Well, I have to go back to my mother's house, drop off my groceries, and help her prepare for my grandmother's arrival."

I nod, "Thank you again for helping me pick up my groceries all over the parking lot, let alone giving me a ride home."

I flash a smile as she speaks, "You're welcome, and now, I have a funny story to tell my family when I get to the house!" Luna chuckles under her breath.

She flashes a warm, beautiful smile as I shake my head thinking about the crazy time. As Luna walks out my door and into the apartment building hallway, her footsteps echo towards the stairs.

I suddenly call out to her from my doorway, "Luna!" she looks over at me near the stairs. "Um...would you like to catch up for lunch or dinner sometime?" I say, asking her out on a date.

Luna laughs slightly with a bright smile on her face. "Sure, I'd like that," her eyes sparkle at me.

I flash a toothy grin, "What time and day are good for you?"

Luna thinks for a moment with her hand resting underneath her chin. "Umm...this Thursday would be good for me in the evening." she walks back to me.

I grab a piece of paper and rip it in half. I write my number down as I give her the other half. Luna writes down her number, and we exchange contact information:

"Here's my number; I'll stop by your apartment at six." She hands me her slip of paper.

I take it and give her my half, "Sounds good to me, but where should we go? I don't know DC very well because I moved here not too long ago." My eyebrows are sparse apart, awaiting her answer.

Luna's eyes light up with a grin, "It's alright; I know where we can go for dinner." she answers with a wink. "I'll see you on Thursday!" she says, leaving me in suspense.

I hesitate to ask her what she has in mind, but I am tongue-tied as time slows down for me.... The most beautiful woman meanders down the stairs and into the sunlight.

CHAPTER FOUR

Spring 1941

"Terrible, just terrible you may stay with us Michael, …I'm sorry about your father, Mr. Adelman; he was a dear friend," says Mr. Dembitz, Emily's father.

Michael, Mr. Dembitz, Mrs. Dembitz, and Emily are all in the parlor of the Dembitz residence. They had listened to Michael's story about his parents.

Mr. Dembitz shallows his breath, "We can't stay here; I'm going to talk with my friend Mr. Färber about arranging a hiding place for us. It's not safe here anymore."

Mrs. Dembitz's eyebrows rise to her husband: "Mr. Färber! Ethan Färber, the Christian pastor?"

Mr. Dembitz paces the floor and rubs the temples upon his forehead. "Yes, that's him. He's been my friend since childhood; he's my most trusted and valued friend." He stops pacing and stares at his wife, "Yes, he's a Christian, and we are Jewish, but I'd rather go to someone I can strongly trust."

Silence fills the entire room. Then, finally, Mrs. Dembitz fiddles with her hands in her lap and speaks, "When will you go talk to him?"

"Tomorrow morning." Mr. Dembitz's eyes never left his wife's.

Mrs. Dembitz turns pale, and her lips sink into her mouth, "In that case, we should get ready to leave."

Mr. Dembitz grits his teeth, "Yes, I agree, but we can't go with our suitcases. We'll look too suspicious for the Nazis." He glares at everyone in the room, "Carry only what you can and leave everything else behind."

Mrs. Dembitz's eyes anchors on her daughter and her voice is stern, "Emily, please take Michael upstairs to the guestroom. He can stay here for the night. We'll hopefully be leaving tomorrow sometime."

There is a dreaded pause; Emily's heart lumps in her chest with anxiety from the discussion. She finally croaks, "Yes, Mama..." she toddles to Michael and grips his hand.

They begin a slow march upstairs as Emily leads Michael to the guestroom. He sits on the bed and weeps at his father's death and for his mother being taken away. Emily sits there next to him, trying to comfort him. She embraces him as Michael's tears stain her blouse. Emily holds him close to her and feels his warm, – shallowed breaths against her chest. He tugs and grips the back of Emily's blouse as his emotions overwhelm him. Emily strokes Michael's hair from the back and sobs with him.

The following morning, Mr. Dembitz returns from talking with his friend Mr. Färber, who arranges a hiding place for the Dembitz family and Michael. Emily is in her room, looking around and choosing what belongings to take. Upon her bed, she sees her most precious teddy bear. It's brown, worn, and frayed from all the attention it received over the years. She wraps her arms around her bear and tightly presses her nose against it. Her face is hot and red as old memories of her bear flash. She was five when her furry companion came to her. Her father had the bear wrapped up in his coat to protect it from the rain. She was in bed, sick with a temperature, when her father presented the bear. She remembered the scent of her father's drenched coat, her father knelt at her bedside, and he pretended the bear was alive. He gripped it in his hand behind its neck, swayed with the bear, and squealed in a high-pitched voice. Emily recalled her father's voice as his words echoed, *'Hello, I'm Alina because you bring the light into my world!'*

When the memory ends…. The emotions from when Emily first sees her bear overwhelm her, and her eyes wander to her clothes on her bed, "Oh, Alina. My dearest bear…I wish I could take you with me…." She kisses her bear and sets it on her bed against her pillow.

Emily stares at her bear, grabs a few pieces of clothing from her bed, and senses Michael standing by her bedroom doorway. Emily holds a top against her chest, turning her head towards him. Michael shifts his body, facing the other way so Emily can dress with as many clothes as she can possibly put on.

"It's okay now; you can come in," says Emily to Michael after a few moments.

As soon as Michael comes in, Mr. Dembitz stumps in, "We have to go now…. Mr. Färber is waiting for us, and he'll be at his old church."

The Dembitz and Michael abandon the house around six-thirty that morning and scuttle to the old church. They all have layers of clothing on because they cannot carry suitcases around with the Nazi patrolmen marching through the streets. Nevertheless, everyone keeps looking forward; they act casual and dare not to stare or get stopped by patrolmen.

Emily is frightened and hears the Nazi patrolmen talking in German to other patrolmen. She squeezes onto Michael's hand grasping it tightly. Holding Emily's hand, Michael strokes his thumb on her palm to soothe her worries.

The Minutes elapse, and the tension becomes hectic; the group hears the soldiers' boots clicking against the ground back and forth. With his peripheral vision, Michael is on guard and can almost hear his own heartbeat. It constantly pumps as he watches the patrolmen. The Jewish star is covered with all the layers of clothes everyone is wearing. Of course, nobody nor the patrolmen know that they are Jews.

Eventually, near the city's edge, the old Christian church stands in the distance where the pastor, Ethan Färber, is waiting for them.

"Frank, great to see you made it here safely.!" Pastor Färber sparks a warm smile with open arms. Then, he saunters to his friend Mr. Dembitz and embraces him with a hug of welcome.

"Thanks, Ethan, for allowing my family to stay within your church," humbly replies Mr. Dembitz. Mr. Dembitz grips his friend's hand while his clasps on top and shakes it.

Pastor Färber grins, "It's my gratitude, Frank! Please come in and let me show you where you are staying."

Pastor Färber pads towards the church. He opens the door, leads them inside, and they pass through the altar. They go to the right and up a stairwell. They walk further down the hall past Pastor Färber's corridor to a wall. The stone wall appears normal until Pastor Färber pulls out a stone brick and a secret passageway magically opens, revealing a flight of stairs.

Everyone ambles up the stairs into a secret room, "This is where you'll be staying; I know this is rather a tiny room, but it will do." Pastor Färber clears his throat, "Now, church services run from eight in the morning until eleven in the morning on Sundays, and we have church sermons during the evenings of the week from six to eight. I must advise you to remain silent and quiet during these times because people can hear you within the church walls. My wife and I will bring you food and supply to live here, along with any news on the war."

"Thank you, Ethan," nods Mr. Dembitz.

The room only has one bed made for two on the left side, and there are no windows. It is all stone walls, and on the right is a condensed bathroom with just a toilet and sink that can only use cold water.

Further to the right of the secret room is a doorway leading to another corridor about half its size. Within the small space is a sleeping bag on the left, ready to be used, a small desk on the right side, and a ladder straight ahead facing the entrance. Up the ladder, there is a wooden hatch door leading into the church's bell tower.

In the bell tower stands the massive bell, shutters all around the tower keeping the area well insulated from the outside world. There is a small empty space in the corner of the bell tower a few feet away from the bell with another sleeping bag set.

This is now everyone's new home. Mr. and Mrs. Dembitz have the bed for two, Emily has the half-sized corridor, and Michael has the corner in the bell tower. Everyone settles in as best they can while Pastor Färber prepares to start his church service.

Eight o'clock comes around the corner, with everyone being more silent than church mice. Mrs. Dembitz, settling in the chair next to the bed, begins knitting a button that fell off one of the articles of clothing while Mr. Dembitz is lying on the bed reading a book he brought with him. Emily is sitting at the desk in the half-sized corridor writing a poem, and Michael is in the bell tower, lying on the sleeping bag staring at the ceiling.

It stays this way throughout the morning; everyone listens to Pastor Färber talking below and the voices of many people that showed up for church. Nobody moves. Everyone remains silent; Mr. Dembitz hands his wife a book after she is done knitting while he reads halfway through his book, Emily writes three poems, and Michael dozes off to sleep every now and then. This is their new way of life. They live in complete silence and are not allowed to move whenever church services start. After church hours, everyone walks and talks, but they can never leave the secret room because of the ultimate fear of discovery.

CHAPTER FIVE

April 19, 2012

"Well, this is it…it's Thursday, finally!" I shout at the top of my lungs, chipper than a jackrabbit on a date! I do a little dance as it's close to six. Luna will arrive at my apartment in due time! I dress in decent clothes; black docker pants, a dark red dress shirt, and a red tie. I tie the necktie in a knot but groan for messing up the length. I roll my eyes, trying to untie it, but it's stuck in its knot.

I catch glimpses of myself in the mirror; I am nice and clean-shaven. Then, five minutes before six, there is a knock at my door, and I stagger over to answer it while fixing my tie. I open the door, and there stands Luna, wearing a lovely dress that matches the color of her eyes and hair.

The dress is jet-black, slim, and the skirt touches fingertip length at her sides, "Hi!" she flashes a bright smile.

My entire body tingles numb, and my eyes are wide at her apparent beauty, "Hi, you look beautiful...." I mumble, soft-spoken.

Luna's brown eyes glow, "Thanks," she says to me.

"So, would you like to come in?" I gesture with my hand inviting her in.

She laughs, "You should fix your collar; it's sticking up."

I pause like a deer in headlights until it clicks, "Oh...." I muffle my breath into an airy chuckle.

I adjust my collar franticly, and my face beets red, "May I?" Luna gently requests.

I stop as I stare into her eyes; she adjusts my collar, "There.... Now, you're ready!"

Her lips crease into a heartwarming smile. "I'd love to come inside, but we should get going. We can't be late for our dinner reservation!" she gestures her hand for me to follow.

My eyebrows pique with curiosity, "A dinner reservation?" I follow her and shut my door, "Where are we going?" I ask as I lock my door.

Luna twirls around to face me and clasps her hands, "I can't tell you; it's a surprise.... You'll have to find out for yourself!"

I sigh, "You really can't tell me?" I jam my hands into my pockets and swirl them around to mellow my excitement.

"No, I can't, and trust me, you'll like it!" Luna and I exit the apartment building.

We pace to her car, and she drives to where our dinner reservation is at seven. In time, we are out of the city and arrive at a small port near the Potomac River.

Luna parks the car, "A dinner boat cruise?"

I whisper in shock, "You didn't have to do this...."

"It's fine, but I thought this would be good, considering you're new to DC!"

Her keys jingle as the car beeps from them inside the ignition. I hear her pull the keys out as I observe the cruise boat. It's pure white and enormous, stretching from one end of the dock to the other. Lights illuminate inside its windows, giving it a tender glow. It's almost as magical and bright as Luna. Excitement brews and grows.... I have never been on a dinner boat cruise before.

Luna and I get out of the car and stroll to the ship for boarding. While boarding, I discover the option for couples to have their picture taken. Luna and I sashay over and stand on the docks in front of the ship. A crew photographer takes our picture. Luna and I smile as I swing my arm around her waist, and she caresses her arm around my shoulder. The camera flashes, and I see spots after the picture is taken.

While walking with Luna up the ramp to get aboard, my feet stumble upon the gap between the ramp and the ship. Various shades of light cloud my vision, and Luna grips my hand. I feel her tugging me along.

"This way, silly…." she says with a chuckle. I hear various voices talking inside, and we are finally aboard the ship. I rub my eyes, trying to get rid of all the colored spots – there are blue, green, and red, purple; too many to mention.

Luna laughs, noticing my hardship, "Are you going to be ok?" she looks at me.

"Yes, I'll be fine," I say as I stare at her, as the colors fade to a faint blur, and Luna's image focuses and blends into my vision like a picture. She is beautiful.

We pad up to the hostess, "Table for two for Braun and Campel," Luna says to the hostess.

The lady looks at the list of reservations, "Ah, yes, right this way, please!" the lady answers.

She grabs menus and leads us to a round table by a window where we can see the outside. A lit candle rests in the center of the table, and the table is set delicately with silver-made silverware. I pull out a chair for Luna to sit on, and I take a seat in the chair across from her at the table.

The lady gives us the two menus as she takes out her notepad and pen. She explains what they have on specials, "Welcome aboard! Our special tonight is Salmon Mediterranean, which is a fresh Alaskan salmon fillet drizzled with citrus, white wine, and dill, served with a fresh vegetable chutney, roasted garlic, and Mediterranean herbs." Her eyes shift between us, and she clicks her pen repeatedly.

Saliva floods my mouth, and I swallow it, "Ah, that sounds wonderful. I'll have that special!"

The hostess stops clicking her pen, stares at her notepad, and writes what I asked for, "Ok, Sir, would you like everything that comes with it?" she chimes, still writing in her notepad.

"Yes, Ma'am!" I exclaim.

She smiles at my choice, "Okay, and how about you, Miss?" she gestures politely.

Luna bites her lips as they sink into her mouth. Her eyes shift side to side, "I'd like to have some white wine, but I haven't made up my mind yet for food." says Luna, still looking through the menu.

"Okay, I'll have someone come back with the bottle of white wine, and if you are interested, we have our grand buffet dinner available, as well!" adds the lady pointing out the buffet.

"Thank you very much," I respond as the hostess nods her head and walks away.

We are silent for a few minutes while Luna looks over the menu. Then we jolt simultaneously as the ship starts moving slowly and sails upon the river, and we laugh together from our jostle. Other people are sitting at tables with a small bar in the corner, and further down is a small music stage.

Soon, a waiter prances over with our bottle of white wine, "Here's your white wine," he says, pouring the wine into thin wine glasses. "Are you ready, my lady?" the waiter gestures to Luna.

"Yes, I'd like the Pasta Primavera," she points.

The waiter writes it down as he studies where Luna's finger pointed, "Would you like the Marinara pasta sauce or Chef's homemade?" he adds, glancing at her.

Luna thinks for a moment, "Hm…what would you recommend? I've never had your pasta."

The waiter clears his throat, "Well, my personal favorite is our Chef's homemade pasta sauce, Ma'am!"

"That would be nice," Luna's eyes wander as if she's thinking.

"Okay, great! Your food will arrive shortly," he recites while taking our menus. "Anything else I can get you?" he asks Luna and me.

"No, thank you," I answer.

"I'm fine," follows Luna.

"Okay, enjoy your time on the cruise!" The waiter strides away to place the order.

I look at Luna and notice she is playing with her necklace, the Star of David.

"When did you get that necklace?" I ask her with curiosity.

Her eyes dart as if I broke her from a trance, "Oh, I've had this necklace since the day I was born; my mother gave it to me. It belonged to her, and she passed it on to me." Luna explains while she pulls the necklace from her neck and glares at it.

"Your family is Jewish?" I add, sipping my wine.

Luna releases her necklace from her grasp, which falls delicately around her neck.

Her eyes focus upon me, "Yes, and so I'm I.... Does it bother you?" she asks as she bites her lip.

"No, not at all. I just wondered," I say to Luna with a smile.

Luna smiles back at me, pleased about my answer, "What about your family?" she asks.

"My family is from Kentucky, and I grew up on a horse farm there. My parents used to race horses for a living, and I grew up Christian." I pinch my fingertips against the stem of my glass.

"Kentucky seems nice. I've never been there, but I love horses which is why I'd like to go there someday!" she says vibrantly.

"Why haven't you gone there?" I inquire as I sip from my glass.

Luna pauses, "I have to stay here in DC to take care of my mother," she sips her wine.

"Is she ill?" I ask Luna while she takes another sip.

"Yes, she has a movement disorder disease. She developed it in her mid-thirties when I was a child...." She explains with her eyes downcast as she taps her finger against the top-bottom part of her glass.

Soon, a young gentleman goes on the music stage and plays a soft, delicate piano tune.

As the man plays, I ask, "Isn't your father there taking care of her? I'm sure with him there, you could go visit the horse country."

Luna shakes her head, and her voice brittles, "No, he left my mother and I when we learned she developed the disease. He just abandoned my mother and I, leaving her to take care of me, and of course, I had to take care of her too!"

I was speechless after she told me about her mother. I continue to listen to her, "My grandmother is over at my mother's house, like I told you before. She's taking care of her while I am here with you tonight. A lot of guys don't date me because of my mother, due to the fact I must take care of her, and I just don't have time to meet someone nice...."

Finally, our food arrives, and the smell delights my senses. The waiter presents our food, "Here's your Alaskan salmon, sir," he says to me, placing the dish in front of me.

"Thank you," I answer.

The waiter sets the pasta in front of Luna, "Your pasta, ma'am," he follows with a grin.

"Thank you," she answers.

"Is everything fine? Do you need anything else?" the waiter asks.

"No, this is great. Thank you!" says Luna stirring her pasta.

The waiter bows his head and leaves. I observe the steam rising from her bowl, and I cut into the salmon, "So why did you move here to DC?" asks Luna swirling the noodles with her fork.

She takes a bite from her pasta as I look at her to answer, "I got a job at a history museum because they found my resume online. They were impressed that I earned my history degree at the top of my class at The University of Kentucky, and so I got hired there. After I got the job, I moved here and rented the small apartment I live in now." I stab the salmon with my fork, bite it, and chew. Eventually, telling her the rest, including how I lost my job and my string of bad luck.

Luna laughs with me, hearing the story of how I got fired along with the bad luck I always seem to have. More time passes, and we finish our dinner a little after eight and leave a tip with the payment of our food for the waiter. Soon, more entertainment on the music stage begins, and many onboard start to party and dance to the music.

We get up from our round table, "Come on, let's go!" she takes my hand after saying this to me.

We edge out of the party, go up the stairs, and onto the ship's deck. Nobody is around due to the party inside; the night sky shines brightly with all the stars gleaming. We lean against the guard rail in awe of the magnificent view above.

Luna's mouth is ajar as she whispers, "Oh, it's so beautiful!" In amazement, we gaze up at the stars. As I gaze up at the stars with her, I feel the wind flowing against me from the ship moving within the Potomac. A moment passes; she and I continue to stare at the stars. I swing my arm around her like a teenage kid would do in a movie theater. Luna jolts from the touch of my arm around her and my hand on her shoulder.

After a few moments, she gently strokes my hand on her shoulder. My breath suspires as I feel her touch. She graces her hand on top of mine while my fingers stroke her shoulder. She continues to tickle the top of my hand delicately with her thumb. Seconds later, she wraps her other arm around my side, pulling me close. She holds my hand on her shoulder and then slowly and comfortably rests her head on my shoulder while we hold hands.

I inhale the scent of her long dark hair, and my heart aches with tender affection:

"Charlie…." whispers Luna softly to me.

We stare face to face, deeply and tenderly, gazing into each other's eyes. I caress her cheek. It's a lost moment, the atmosphere is emotionally tense, and I sense the strength of our emotions growing. I shut my eyes, anchor my neck, and feel her lips against mine for only a second. We look at each other again, stare, and her eyes sparkle. I kiss her, and our lips lock together for the first time.

CHAPTER SIX

Summer 1942

"Emily, what has been going on with you and Michael?" asks Mrs. Dembitz resting her hands against her waist.

Emily crosses her arms, "What do you mean, Mama, is something wrong?"

Mr. Dembitz firms his jaw, "No, nothing is wrong…. Your mother and I are just wondering what the deal is with you spending so much time with him in the bell tower."

Emily bites her lip firmly, "I like his company, and he likes mine. Is something wrong with that?"

Mr. Dembitz shakes his head, "No, it's fine. We just want you to be careful."

Emily frowns at her parents and abruptly speaks, "Be careful? Michael is a good man, and besides, he likes my smile!"

Mr. Dembitz rubs his finger against his chin, "That's what we mean, Em…. We want you to be careful with how you and he are attracted to each other!"

Emily bats her eyes in confusion, "So, I can't be around him?"

Mrs. Dembitz purses her lips into a thin line, "No, darling, you can be around him, of course; we just advise you to be careful with your feelings."

Mr. Dembitz interjects: "We've noticed how you and he look at each other since our time spent here over the last year."

Emily rolls her eyes, "Well, I like it, and I like him!" Emily storms to the bell tower.

After Emily leaves her parents, they look at each other, hoping she can understand what they are trying to tell her. It's July of forty-two, and the group has been hiding from the German Nazis since May of forty-one. Pastor Färber and his wife are still taking care of everyone in hiding. They give them donations from the church, such as food, clothing, and updates on the outside world. Pastor Färber, on his days off, tutors Michael and Emily. He educates them so that they can continue their education on certain days of the week.

Emily visits Michael often and lightly knocks on the wooden hatch door. Eventually, she taps upon the wooden hatch, and Michael opens it, "Hey, is this a bad time?"

Michael observes Emily hunched, fiddling with her hands, and biting her lip. Her neck anchors up to him like a lost kitten.

Michael places his math homework from Pastor Färber aside, "No, it's not a bad time; are you alright?" asks Michael with a comforting smile.

Emily smirks at Michael's smile, but it suddenly dissipates into a despondence: "It's just my parents," mutters Emily gripping onto a wooden peg from the ladder.

Michael tilts his head as a gesture, inviting Emily into the bell tower. They sit cross-legged next to each other in the small, spaced corner, "They are concerned about us spending so much time together...." Emily's eyes drift as she says this.

"Do you think it's a bad thing us spending too much time together?" asks Michael.

"No, of course not!" Emily's head bolts quickly.

Their eyes follow each other, "They want me to be careful with my feelings, but do you believe it's a bad thing us spending so much time?" asks Emily wanting to know Michael's opinion. Michael thinks for a moment and wraps his arm around Emily.

"No, I don't think it's a bad thing, but we shouldn't rush into anything. We should take our time."

There is a moment of silence as Emily finally speaks, "Michael, may I ask you a personal question?"

Michael's heart jilts, and he swallows the lump in his throat, "Sure."

Emily's eyes shift to the floor and back at him, "During school or any time before we came into hiding, have you ever kissed a girl before?"

Michael takes a moment to look at Emily. Then, his breathing shallows, "No, I've never kissed a girl, to be honest…. I've always been the quiet one and too shy to kiss a girl."

Emily chuckles under her breath with a warm grin at him, "A boy kissed me one day, but I guess it doesn't really count, considering it was on the cheek. Before going to the Jewish school, I was being made fun of at school by a random group of kids just because I'm Jewish. A young boy saw the group of kids making fun of me, and he told them to leave me alone. The group of kids just walked away thinking they were better than him, and I began to cry because the crude jokes deeply hurt me. Then, the boy turned to me, kissing me on my cheek, saying, 'don't worry, you're beautiful just the way you are.' He made me smile and feel better about myself, but then he moved away to Switzerland, and I never saw him again."

Emily pauses, and her eyes gleam through Michael's soul, "You were always quiet though, during that time at the public school we used to go to."

Michael parts his mouth with a little smile, and his breath deflates, "I was scared to come up to you; I didn't have the nerve."

Emily squints her eyes at him, puzzled, "Why were you scared to talk to me?" she asked.

"Because I liked you, and I was afraid you wouldn't feel the same way I feel about you," answers Michael.

"Awe, Michael...." mewls Emily with a smile: "I had no idea you liked me before we switched to the Jewish school."

Michael rubs his hands against his thighs nervously, "I've always liked you.... I could see something special in you when I first saw you," says Michael.

"You think I'm special?" she asks him.

"Yes, you'll always be special to me!" Emily embraces Michael after those words, and they hold onto one another for a while.

For a few seconds more, they are lost in each other's eyes and press their lips together for a tender kiss.

Later that night, after the church service from below, everyone is dead asleep. Suddenly, everyone is woken up by the loud sound of the church's front doors being pushed open. Everyone lies still, not trying to move. They don't want to be discovered. Everyone listens to footsteps below. It staggers throughout the church's altar, smashing and throwing belongings within. The stranger going through the church sounds like they are searching for something.

Everyone dreads when they hear this person searching, knocking things over, and looming up the stairwell. Everyone listens to each and individual footstep coming up the stairwell. It echoes throughout the church. The mysterious stranger is in the hallway and now ambles inside Pastor Färber's corridors. Soon, Pastor Färber's belongings in his corridor are thrown, tossed, and scattered all over the floor of his room.

Still, everyone keeps silent and motionless, praying they won't be discovered. Everyone's hearts tremble with fear, like an omen of evil will come to get them.

The mysterious being is in the hallway again. It lurches farther down past Pastor Färber's corridor. Finally, the footsteps halt in front of the stone wall, the hidden entrance to where everyone is hiding. A few moments of complete silence pass as if the drop of a pin can be heard.

Suddenly, a loud noise wails and pounds against the stone four times. Mr. Dembitz, with his wife on the bed, holds her for comfort. Meanwhile, in the bell tower, Michael hears the soft, frightful sound of Emily's silent tears in the half-sized corridor below him. Then, after the fourth hard hit against the stone wall, it becomes utterly silent again.

Soon, everyone listens to the mysterious visitor's feet shifting away from the stone wall for a second. However, the mysterious visitor's presence still looms by the stone wall like a ghostly apparition.

Not even a minute later, the mysterious visitor's footsteps reverberate away from the wall. Then, it goes back down the stairwell. The unwanted visitor's footsteps still haunt the church's first floor. The unwanted visitor has one last look around. About eight minutes elapse, and everyone's ears internally buzz at the mysterious visitor's footsteps still stalking the church. Eventually, whoever this visitor is, slams the church doors behind them.

Hours later, Pastor Färber and his wife arrive at their church in the early morning. They notice what happened within the church as they dash up the stairwell opening the secret stone wall.

"Frank, this is Pastor Färber. Is everyone alright?!" yells the pastor. Mr. Dembitz appears at the entrance of the secret room. His eyes catch delight in seeing his dear friend standing at the door.

"Yes, everyone is fine. However, we heard an unwanted visitor last night. This mysterious person came searching for something by the sound of how they looked around, throwing everything. They did not find us, though." stated Mr. Dembitz.

"Good, thank God; praise the Lord!" exclaims Pastor Färber.

He scuffles up the stairwell with his wife behind him, "My wife and I need to talk to you and everyone. We have news to share!"

Pastor Färber and his wife enter the secret room. Mr. Dembitz goes farther inside the room for Pastor Färber and his wife to come in and give the news. Emily and Michael hear Pastor Färber and his wife coming in. They rush down to listen to the report.

Everyone is in the secret room as Pastor Färber announces the news: "It appears that a robber came into the church last night and stole some of the donations from the church and its food. I don't think the robber knew anything about you all, and the fact you're all still safe is a testament to that. In other news, it's not looking too well.... I know I must give you hope, but I also must be realistic about what's happening. The Gestapo are rallying Jews like flies, which has become more violent. It's true what everyone is saying about Hitler's Nazi concentration camps. Many Jews are being sent to death and labor camps, captured by the gray trucks, and then transported onto trains. From what I know, the trains run to these camps like Auschwitz. Families are separated, chosen to go to a labor camp, or sent to the gas chambers. In these chambers, as I have heard, the Nazis send many into the room in large numbers.

The victims, I hear, are forced to undress, men, women, and children alike, and given the impression that they would be given a shower after the long train ride to the camp. I have heard countless rumors that there are no windows, just overhead showers in multitudes. Once inside, instead of water coming out of the showerheads, a gas is released, killing all those inside. I do not know what type of gas, but things aren't looking too bright. I surely hope and pray to God that the Allies will end this war soon."

A complete moment of silence fills the room, and everyone stares at one another in absolute shock at the words that come out of Pastor Färber's mouth. Mrs. Dembitz turns pale as a desolate statue; Mr. Dembitz's hands quiver as he squeezes them into fists like a stress ball. Emily's eyes are horrified, wide with disdain and dread.

Anger seethes into Michael's demeanor. He grits his teeth and presses his lip into a thin line, "What about everyone that Emily and I went to the Jewish school with? Have they been taken?" asks Michael.

Pastor Färber's wife edges forward, "While going to work the other day, I saw many gray trucks parked near the school and taking the children away," she answers.

Mrs. Färber croaks, "A Nazi officer saw me looking at what was going on, and he told me to keep moving, and so I did; there was nothing I could do."

Michael stands there in silence, taking everything in. Emily weeps, and tears in her eyes flood from hearing the news. Mrs. Dembitz is speechless, she acts like she is in another world, and Mr. Dembitz nods his head with a heavy heart. Pastor Färber goes up to his friend Mr. Dembitz and gives him a comforting hug.

It's silent that night. Nobody says anything to one another. Everyone is still in shock about the news. Church runs its normal time that night, six to eight, and later, everyone drifts to sleep. It's the middle of the night, around one in the morning, and Michael bolts from his slumber. The wooden hatch door opens. He peers through the opening and sees Emily weeping. She huddles forth into the room.

"I'm sorry to startle you like this in the middle of the night. I had an awful nightmare about my best friend, Hannah.... She was in one of those camps that Pastor Färber told us about. I'm so scared...." she cries in a soft, hoarse voice.

"You can sit with me if you'd like." He pats the sleeping bag.

Emily toddles over to him and sits beside him on the sleeping bag. A few moments pass, and Emily talks a bit about her dream.

"I saw Hannah in striped pajamas weeping in pain! She called my name for help. Her hair was gone; she looked like she hadn't eaten anything in days or months. She was starving to death. I'm so afraid, Michael. Do you think Hannah is at one of those camps? I don't want to go to that place...." Emily weeps more and her breath shallows.

Michael embraces her and holds her in his arms. He comforts her, "Sometimes, I think it's just easier to give up.... Sometimes, I wish I wasn't Jewish." muffles Emily against Michael's body.

Michael tugs Emily closer and says, "Emily, you can't give up yourself because HaShem hasn't given up on you. He'll never give up on you, so please don't give up on him!"

Emily lifts her head as the tears stream and rolls down her cheeks.

"Then why is HaShem letting this happen?" she mewls. "HaShem didn't let this happen, Emily; it's that omen, Adolf Hitler. He's the one to blame. He's the one that has gotten everyone in this mess, and I pray that HaShem will strike him down for it!"

Michael grits his teeth as Hitler's shouting voice from the radio echoes in his mind. Then, as one of Hitler's speeches rings in his head, memories of Michael's parents flash simultaneously. The times they had, the laughter, their vacations in Holland and Geneva visiting friends and family.

Emily croaks as her voice breaks Michael's reveries: "I don't want to be captured, Michael. Every day and night, I'm so afraid that we'll get discovered!" Emily squeezes onto Michael as if death is approaching her.

Michael chimes, "Yes, I feel the same, Emily, but no matter what happens, you'll never be alone. I made a promise to you that day on the school stairs, and a promise is forever, for better or worse." Michael's fingers trickle through Emily's hair and the back of her hot neck.

Emily and Michael stare at one another with Emily's tears still rolling down her face. "I love you, Michael," whispers Emily softly as she moves to kiss him. Michael and Emily's lips lock together, and at that very moment, everything changes.

CHAPTER SEVEN

April 23, 2012

Hot diggity dog that night with Luna is beyond words, and I honestly can't say or describe how amazing it was! It was so magical. I think it's something I'll never forget for the rest of my life. Here I am, convinced I have the worst luck on the freaking planet when I first came to DC. First, with losing my job at the history museum, losing my car, and how clumsy I am in life. Well, all I can say is that something positive came out of it! I met Luna! I returned home to my tiny apartment that night with a smile on my face. This excitement with Luna and this new relationship almost makes me forget about the ring!

I have tried tirelessly to find its owner but to no avail. I've tried Craigslist, Facebook advertisements, and even the old Myspace, but nothing. Just bidders who are interested in pawning the ring…. Screw that! Perhaps Ancestry can help? I'll have to investigate it! I vigorously research Michael Luke Adelman's name but find nothing. No marriage certificate on the exact date. There are other Adelmans, but none match the date on the ring. This is upsetting me – driving me mad! I glare back at the window. It's black outside; it's midnight. I need to focus on finding a job. I decide to go to bed and try my luck again in filling out job applications.

The following morning my phone rings. I lie in bed when it continues to ring. I stretch over and attempt to grip the phone from its hook, but my hand fails and plummets.

It rings, and finally, I answer it, "Hello?" I mutter hoarsely.

"Hello, is this Charlie Parker Campel?" asks a man on the phone.

My eyes bat from the sleepiness, "Why yes, this is he…." I mumble back.

"Good day to you, Mr. Campel; I'm Ryan Hoggins, The National Civil War Museum manager. I have gone through the application you sent in. I am wondering if you can come in for an interview later today at three this afternoon?" said the man on the phone.

I bolt up quickly as excitement takes over from what I have just heard. I almost choke, "Um… uh… yes, Mr. Hoggins, I can come to the museum at three!" I rush over to my closet, the other half of the phone slams upon the ground but is still connected.

"Sounds good. When you arrive, talk to the lady at the front desk, and I'll see you when you get here," adds Hoggins.

"Thank you, sir!" We disconnect. I hang up the phone and check the clock to see what time it is, "It's one in the afternoon! I slept in a bit more than usual; dang it!"

I scurry towards my bathroom but trip over my shoes that are nearby. I hit my face on the floor, "ouch, ow, ow, ugh!" I groan and spring up.

I dress quickly – blazer, red dress shirt, and tie. I comb my hair – ready to go; no – dress pants! I tuck my shirt in, adjust my belt, and dart for my black dress shoes. I push my feet inside, and I dash out my door! My apartment keys jingle, my cheeks bulge air, and they deflate a growl, "Blah, need to lock the door; sheesh!" My feet slide, and my body slams against my door. I scuffle my keys, breathing wildly, and sigh in the pleasure of my door locking. I bolt out to the city to get a taxicab.

"Taxi!" I shout, observing one ahead.

A few feet closer to the taxi, another man snatches my cab. My mouth is ajar, but before I can say anything, the taxi drives away, and I stomp my foot against the sidewalk. My eyes catch a glimpse of another taxicab a few blocks down, and I hoof it over there. I make it as the taxi driver sees me.

"Need a ride?" he calls to me.

"Yes, Sir!" I shout breathlessly. I shove myself in the back.

"Where to?" he asks while resetting his payment meter on the dashboard.

"The National Civil War Museum," I demand.

"The national what?" he cuffs his hand around his ear.

"The National Civil War Museum," I say again.

"Fort Ward Museum? Speak up, son. I can't hear you!" My patience grows thin.

"The National Civil War Museum!" I yell at him.

"Oh, The National Civil War Museum; I know right where that is!" The taxi driver nods his head. I groan and bite my lip.

"I'm sorry, sir; you'll have to speak up. Unfortunately, my hearing is not that great," he adds as he starts to drive.

Soon, his cell phone rings loudly with its volume all the way up. He flips his phone, "Ello!" he buzzes very loudly.

There is a moment of pause, "Ah, Zach attack, my flack lack! What's going on, dude?" he blares to his friend on the phone.

The taxi driver is steering with one hand while having his cell phone in the other. It's up to his ear as he continues driving. The driver talks loudly and brassy; I hear his conversation a bit, "Ah, no way, dude, really? When is he coming into town?" he inquires. "Ah, man…. We'll totally get together for some beers, man!" booms the driver.

From where I am sitting in the back, I cannot tell if the driver is paying attention to the road or not. So, I buckle my seat belt, for I feel uneasy, "Ah, nothing much, man, just working right now! I'm driving a young man to the National Civil War Museum," clatters the driver.

I glance over at the pay meter; It's almost twenty dollars! I check my pockets to see if I have enough money – no money! I panic frantically, patting all my pockets to make sure, and I have nothing.

"Oh, Jesus…" I murmur under my breath. I bang my head slightly against the car window.

Suddenly, I catch the driver swerving into the wrong turning lane. A car is coming right at him. "Oh, sweet mother of ganja!" screams the taxi driver.

The taxicab hastes into the correct lane, and I smash my head against the window from its speeding turn. The car horn wails at the taxi driver as he honks back.

"Snollygoster, people driving these days!" blares the taxi driver wailing his fist.

He grips the wheel quickly with his other hand, still holding his phone. Then He tells his buddy about what happened, "Ah, nah, man… I'm fine. It's just some snollygoster–pillock coming at me, driving with stupidity!" the taxi driver groans at his buddy on the phone.

From the taxi driver's tone, I assume he thinks it's not his fault for what almost happened.

"Listen, man! I'll catch you later!" he pauses, and I see the paying meter reads twenty-five dollars.

"Have a good one. Bye," he says to his buddy and hangs up.

"You alright, buddy?" his eyes are wide as he glares at me.

My hand rubs the side of my head, "Yeah, I'll be fine…. Just get me there safely." I squeeze my eyes shut.

"Don't worry, man, you're in good hands!" he grins with a mighty smile.

Suddenly, he halts the vehicle from traffic, slowing down, "This is why; I hate DC sometimes…." The taxi driver pats a drum-joke punchline rhythm on his steering wheel.

I lean back in my seat and slam my palm against my face.

"I'm sorry, dude, we could be here for a while. I remember the last time I got stuck like this, and it took two hours for me to start moving again!" he laughs, "I was hotter than a firecracker lit at both ends!"

This is the last thing I want to hear from this guy. I think I stand corrected about my luck…this is just a nightmare! I glare over at my watch on my wrist; it ticks at one-forty-five. The car slowly goes from time to time as I keep my eyes between my watch and the payment meter. *"This can't be happening. Why me, why me?"*

My brain is a rapid tornado. It's like this for I don't know how long until I look at my watch again; it's now two in the afternoon! The payment meter reads twenty-nine dollars, and I hear the taxi driver's stomach growl.

"Oh man," he moans.

He squeezes his stomach with one of his hands and grips the car's steering wheel. Suddenly, the taxi driver rips a loose fart. It pulls long and loud.

"Oh, that hurt!" bellows the taxi driver.

The cab reeks of his gaseous fumes, and the smell wallows in the backseat. My nose whiffs the stench, and it smells like burnt, stale, cheesy nachos.

The fumes of his bowels are in my mouth; I taste them. I shield my mouth and face with my hand.

"Wheew, holy crapola, manlula! I must stay away from that Mexican Restaurant I always go to downtown!" The taxi driver rolls his window down, and I follow his lead.

The taxi driver snorts from his fart while I shake my head, thinking, *'can this get any worse, God?'*

The taxi driver cuffs one of his hands against his mouth. His hand mimics a radio speaker, and he muffles his voice like static, "the skunk is leaving the barn; I repeat, the skunk is leaving the barn!"

After his words, I receive my answer to the question in my mind earlier.

"Oh, air biscuits!" hoots the taxi driver holding his stomach again, "I got barbarians at the gate!" he caterwauls out loud.

I hit the back of my head against the seat, roll my eyes, and shut them, for that is something I really do not need to hear.

I reopen my eyes and study my watch; it's now two-fifteen! I worry, and my mind races faster than horses on a racetrack as I see the payment meter now up to thirty-two dollars.

"Come on!" roars the taxi driver at the slow-moving traffic, "I have to chop logs!"

Finally, the traffic moves, and the taxi driver floors the pedal to my destination. We arrive at the National Civil War Museum, and the taxi driver parks his car in the parking lot. I observe the price I owe him; thirty-six dollars and forty-two cents. Also, the time on my watch displays two-thirty. He interjects when I am about to tell him that I don't have any money.

"Listen, I know you must pay me, but I really gotta go! So, I'll go into the museum with you, and I can use their restroom. You wait for me!"

We get out of the car. The taxi driver lollops to the entrance. I rush after him and say, "Listen, sir, I have an interview at three. Can you wait until then?" I ask.

"Yeah, sure, whatever!" He panics and whips the museum doors wide open. I hear his footsteps streak against the floors as I go to the front desk and introduce myself to the lady.

"Hi, I'm here to see a Ryan Hoggins," my hands press against the edge of the desk.

The receptionist types away at her keyboard, "Hmm…oh, what is it in regard to?" Her eyes never stray from the computer; they do not even bat a wink.

"Mr. Hoggins called me about a position – I'm Charlie Campel."

The lady never looks at me; she clicks away at the keys, "Mr. Hoggins will be right with you in a moment."

She strokes a few more keys with one hand while picking up the phone.

"Thank you," I say, standing there drumming my fingers.

"Ok, I'll let him know…" she sets the phone on its hook, "Mr. Hoggins is on his way."

As she had said this, Hoggins shows up, "Charlie Campel?" he tilts his head at me with a beige folder in his hand.

"Yes, that's me!" I walk to him and shake his hand.

Hoggins grips my hand, "Follow me, sir," he escorts me to his office. We saunter to his office, and he and I sit across from each other.

Hoggins takes out my application, briefly scanning it over. "Mr. Campel, your resume and application are impressive; graduating from the top of your class with a solid history degree at The University of Kentucky, and yet you state here that you got fired from your last job working at a history museum here in DC. So, what happened?" his eyebrows sparse with intimidation.

I explain my story to him; how I got fired from the history museum I used to work at.

"That's the funniest thing I've ever heard! Yes, I've heard that the manager where you used to work is a very unpleasant man to work with. But the next time you lose your keys in an exhibit, please notify me," smirks Hoggins.

"Sir?" I rise as I connect the dots in my head.

"Yes, Mr. Campel, I would love for you to work at this history museum! I can use more people like you that have an excellent record of history on their hands." He shows his hand for a handshake.

"Yes, sir.... I'd love to work here as soon as possible!" I shake his hand firmly.

"Good. In that case, can you start work tomorrow morning? I need another tour guide to work in the mornings; we normally have many people coming in around that time." Hoggins says, crossing his arms.

Without hesitation, I say, "Yes, sir. I can do that for you. I won't let you down!"

Hoggins nods as he shows me to the door, "Great, I'll see you tomorrow morning at seven! Your shift will end at two in the afternoon," he opens his office door.

"Sounds great. See you tomorrow!" I exit his office.

The door shuts. I jump with excitement and with a smile on my face. The taxi driver is waiting for me by the front desk.

"Well, I see the interview went great with the look on your face. Now, where's my money?" he flashes his hand, rubbing his fingertips.

"I don't have any money, sir. I didn't realize it until we got stuck in traffic."

Silence. The taxi driver's face beets red; he gnashes his teeth, almost livid, "You owe me!" he grunts in anger, trying not to shout.

"I know I do…I can get you the money at my bank, and if you drive me there, I'll give you the added-on charge, including if you drop me off where you picked me up," I bargain with him.

He thinks, rubbing his chin for a moment while doing the math in his head, "That's a total of fifty dollars!" he concludes.

"Then, fifty dollars it is!" I shake his hand.

"Alright, deal. Let's go!"

We stroll together toward the exit. While we are leaving, I catch a glimpse of the janitor going into the men's room with a plunger….

The taxi driver drives me to my bank, and I withdraw fifty dollars out of my account. He plays and taps all his fingers upon seeing the money. He takes me back into the city, where he picked me up, and I give him his fifty dollars. He smiles, waves his hand, and drives away. As I sashay to my apartment, I jump up and down with joy to start my new job. Suddenly, while striding up the stairway in the hall, my phone in my apartment rings. I rush over to answer it.

"Hello?" I answer breathlessly.

"Hey!" says a voice.

My brain clicks; it's Luna calling.

"Hey, how are you?" I ask her with a smile.

"I'm fine. I am wondering if you'd like to come over on Friday for dinner. My mom and grandmother will be here, and you can meet them!"

My heart bursts with radiance and excitement, "I'd love to. What time?" I scour my place for a writing utensil and paper.

"I can pick you up at six-thirty, and it will be seven by the time we get to the house." I grasp a pen and crinkle an envelope from an old paper bill, "Yeah, that sounds great. I'll be off work by two. So, that's plenty of time!"

I scribble *Friday; six-thirty* as a reminder.

"You got a new job?" she squeaks loudly with surprise.

"Yes, I got a call from the National Civil War Museum manager to come in for an interview!" I tell Luna the rest of my crazy story and going to the interview.

CHAPTER EIGHT

Autumn 1942

"Emily, you've been in there for a while; are you alright?" asks Mrs. Dembitz, knocking on the bathroom door within the secret room.

There is no response from Emily, just silence as the door finally opens. Emily scuttles out slowly with her hand over her mouth. She places her hand down at her side, "Yes, Mama…I'm fine."

Her eyes falter at the ground, remaining downcast, and she mooches into the half-sized corridor.

Mr. Dembitz approaches his wife and whispers, "Marion, anything?"

Mrs. Dembitz never speaks a word. She bites her lip, shakes her head, and ambles away. Mr. Dembitz's eyebrows pique, and his fingers rub against his forehead. Emily's parents notice something is going on with their daughter…. She has been quieter than usual. Michael notices, too, that Emily hasn't visited him as much. She avoids him despite the small spaces. She sleeps more, isolates herself in the half-sized corridor, and pretends she sleeps. Michael desires to know—he thinks he has done something at first, but he shakes his head and encourages himself to talk to her. He edges down from the bell tower and knocks on the hatch door.

Emily peers slightly at the crack between the wall and hatch, "Do you have a moment?" asks Michael.

Emily opens the wooden hatch door, "Sure," she croaks.

Michael reaches out his hand, and Emily grasps it. She pads up the bell tower with Michael. Michael allows Emily room, and they sit down in the small-spaced corner.

After they sit down, Michael speaks.

"Emily, what's going on? I notice you've been more quiet than usual. It's not like yourself," says Michael with concern in his voice.

Emily stays silent and looks into Michael's eyes. They are compassionate—warm, but her eyes lower down to the floor.

"What's wrong?" he asks once more, wrapping his arm around her.

Pausing, she stares at Michael and groans, but it's broken by her shallowed breath.

"I'm pregnant, Michael," she finally tells him.

Michael is dumbfounded. He sits there in silence. He looks around, not knowing what to say, "Are you certain?" he chokes.

"Yes, I am certain…. I've missed my period, and I've been having morning sickness."

Michael's mouth is ajar.

"Oh, wow…" he adds, not knowing what else to say.

Emily snatches and clutches Michael's hand.

"Michael, I don't know what to do. It will only be a matter of time until my parents find out. I don't know what to do." Emily shudders at Michael for an answer.

"We have to let your parents know; the sooner, the better," says Michael.

"I don't know, Michael. I'm scared to tell them. I have so many mixed emotions about this. I'm happy that I'll be having a child; it's a wonderful feeling, but at the same time, I know of all times, this is not the time to have a child. What will my parents say or do? What will happen nine months from now—Will we still even be here?" she trembles.

"I don't know, Emily, but I feel for right now, it's best to tell your parents. We don't know what the future will bring. We just have to live and do the best we can now to prepare for the future," resolves Michael holding onto Emily's hand.

Michael stares into Emily's eyes and caresses her cheek.

"Emily, I'll do everything in my power to take care of you and our child. I am overwhelmed – I can't really express this moment now. I would have never imagined this happening, but having a child with a woman that a man loves with all of his heart, is the greatest feeling a man could ever feel."

Emily strokes Michael's hand that is upon her cheek.

"Will you be there when I tell my parents?" she asks, frightened and afraid.

"Yes, I will be there for you and take responsibility for what has happened between you and I." Michael kisses Emily.

Michael and Emily plod down from the bell tower, through the half-sized corridor, and into the secret room to tell Emily's parents the news. Michael and Emily toddle, holding hands.

"Mama, Papa," murmurs Emily.

"Yes, sweetheart…. What's wrong?" replies Mr. Dembitz with his wife.

"Michael and I have something to tell you… Please, don't get mad; it's the last thing I need right now because it's hard enough to tell you this…."

Emily tightly holds Michael's hand. A moment of dreaded silence fills the room.

"I'm...having a child…." Emily finally says to her parents.

Emily's mother stares – point blank, and shrouds her hand over her mouth. Emily's father sits up, turns around, and shirks his body away to absorb everything he hears.

Michael steps forward.

"I apologize, Mr. and Mrs. Dembitz; it just happened…."

Bitter anger seethes inside Mr. Dembitz. He violently whirls around to face Michael, "It *just* happened? So, what are you going to do now? What are we going to do now since we're here when we can hardly take care of ourselves!? Now, there's a baby on the way? You two aren't even married, and now you're going to have a child!

Furthermore, your mother and I advised you, Emily, about your feelings. Of course, we didn't want this to happen, at least not now. But it's too late now...." Mr. Dembitz paces back and forth, his breathing unnerved.

Michael gulps but stands firm, "I understand, Mr. Dembitz, but I love Emily with all my heart. Yes, we're not married, and yes, I know this is not the right time, but it happened! We can't change that, so we must be responsible adults instead of quarreling about it!"

Mr. Dembitz stops, rubs the temples upon his forehead, and looks at his wife. She stares back at him and nods her head.

"You love my daughter; would you forever be at her side?" asks Mr. Dembitz, cooler and calmer.

Michael's eyes never stray from Mr. Dembitz's gaze, "Yes, forever and always," replies Michael giving a straight answer.

"Emily, do you love Michael; will you always love him forever?" asks Mrs. Dembitz, finally to her daughter.

"Yes, I love Michael with all my heart. I will always cherish him, Mama." Emily also gives a straight answer.

Emily's parents shift their eyes to each other.

"I suggest we talk to Pastor Färber to see if we can fit in a secret wedding sometime soon then, if that's what you two would like to do?" suggests Mr. Dembitz.

Mr. Dembitz's eyes focus on Emily and Michael after his words.

Mrs. Dembitz interjects: "We can't force you two to get married. It's not our choice; it is up to you. We just want what's best."

Michael and Emily look at one another, and Emily nods her head. Then, Michael turns to Emily, reaches for her hand, and they face Emily's parents.

"Yes, we believe that's the right thing to do," finishes Michael.

That evening Pastor Färber visits the secret room giving small rations of potatoes and bread. Everyone tells him the news of Emily's pregnancy and that Emily and Michael wish to get married. Pastor Färber tells everyone he can arrange a secret wedding, but it has to be a day early in the morning. He also offers to make Emily and Michael wedding rings for their everlasting vows. The day is set for September 20, 1942, which gives Pastor Färber time to prepare and make the rings.

The weeks pass, and the day finally approaches.

Everyone dresses in the best clothes they have. Pastor Färber prepares the rings in time, and he conducts the ceremony. Pastor Färber's wife silently and swiftly brings her camera to the church and takes a picture of the soon-to-be-wedded couple. Everyone is at the altar that early September morning as Pastor Färber begins:

"Dearly beloved, we are gathered here today to witness the eternal love and the forever-lasting vows between Michael Luke Adelman and Emily Sarah Dembitz. We hope, Lord, that you, with your everlasting love and spirit, will forever bless these two couples in the years to come. In your presence, dear God, my Lord, in your eyes, everyone is equal no matter what religion because these are your children, my Lord. You, the creator of this earth and your children. We are here because of your will and, most of all, your eternal love. So, let us show your love through the strong bonded love of one Michael Luke Adelman and Emily Sarah Dembitz," finishes Pastor Färber with a pause.

Pastor Färber looks at the young couple as they hold hand-in-hand. They stare at one another in a most tender gaze. The light through the stained-glass windows shines their unique colors, and the morning light blends upon the newly wedded couple's faces.

Mr. Dembitz walks up with Emily's ring and stands behind Michael.

"Do you, Michael Luke Adelman take Emily Sarah Dembitz to be your lovely, wedded wife, through sickness and health, for richer or poorer, till death does you part?"

"I do," confirms Michael.

Emily's eyes sparkle with light, and Mr. Dembitz holds Emily's ring next to the groom.

"Please place this ring on the hand of your beloved as the eternal symbol in which you promise to carry your oath for better or worse," says Pastor Färber.

Michael takes Emily's ring from Mr. Dembitz's hand, and Emily's father stoops down from the altar. He gracefully sweeps Emily's hand with the ring in his other.

"I, Michael Luke Adelman, take you, Emily Sarah Dembitz, to be my lawfully wedded wife, through sickness, and health, for richer or poorer, and till death do us part." Michael slips the ring onto Emily's finger.

"Do you, Emily Sarah Dembitz, take Michael Luke Adelman as your lawfully wedded husband, through sickness and health, for richer or poorer, till death do you part?" asked Pastor Färber.

Mrs. Dembitz, Emily's mother, sauntered behind Emily and held Michael's ring in her hand.

"I do," confirms Emily, staring into Michael's eyes.

Michael's dimples show, and his eyes bask in the morning light.

"Then, please take this ring to the hand of your beloved as the eternal symbol in which you promise to carry your oath for better or worse."

Emily takes Michael's ring from her mother, and Mrs. Dembitz stoops down from the altar.

"I, Emily Sarah Dembitz, take you, Michael Luke Adelman, to be my lawfully wedded husband, through sickness and health, for richer or poorer, for better or worse," states Emily caressing Michael's hand. Then with the ring in her other hand, she slips the ring onto Michael's finger.

"By the powers vested in me, and through the eyes of the Lord, I now pronounce you husband and wife!"

Michael and Emily smile at each other and share a kiss. They are finally married, and Emily and Michael turn to face everyone after the kiss.

Pastor Färber's wife captures a photo of the new Mr. and Mrs. Adelman. After the brief ceremony, everyone dwells back in the secret room with the same old fear.

CHAPTER NINE

Winter 1942

Emily is four to five months into her pregnancy. Hanukkah arrives during the winter for the family. Mrs. Dembitz, during the time when everyone took what they needed for their solitude, nabbed their family's Candelabrum before everyone went into hiding. Each of the eight nights of Hanukkah, Mr. Dembitz lights the middle candle first after Pastor Färber's church sermons are finished, and the congregation below leaves for the night. On the first night, Mr. Dembitz places a candle on the rightmost position of their menorah, holds it, and everyone whispers the three blessings.

After reciting blessings, the shamash middle candle is lit. Mr. Dembitz grabs the center candle and kindles the flame to light the first candle he placed earlier. When he lights the first candle, he sets the middle candle back in its original place. Everyone softly sings the hymn,

"Ma'oz Tzur," as quietly as they can, and small gifts are exchanged after. This process of kindling one induvial candle continues during the eight nights of Hanukkah and lighting a different candle on the menorah. Mr. Dembitz places the candles right to the left, lights them with the shamash left to right, whispers two blessings, and sets the shamash in its original place. Afterward, everyone sings as silently as they can. They sing different Hanukkah songs and exchange small gifts.

On the final night, Emily receives a gift from Michael that she will never forget and always treasure.

"This is for you, Emily," says Michael.

Everyone sits around the table, and the menorah is placed in the center. Emily's hand shields her mouth, and her eyes are wide.

"Oh, Michael, it's so beautiful!" she squeaks gleefully.

In Michael's hand is a necklace with the pendant of the Star of David. It has six single tiny diamonds on the endpoints of the star.

Emily ladles the necklace and glances down at it in the palm of her hand. Her eyes sparkle at the diamonds on it.

"What are these diamonds on here for?" she putters softly.

Michael grins, "Those six diamonds you see represent you, your father, mother, me, our baby, and the sixth represents our future. So, no matter where you are in this world, we'll always be with you!"

Emily clasps the necklace in the palm of her hand, bolts over to Michael, and embraces him. Michael kisses Emily on her cheek, and Emily turns to her parents with a smile. Both of her parents smile back.

"Can you help me put it on?" she gestures to Michael behind her.

"Sure," he says, adjusting his posture.

Emily grips the necklace's chain around her neck, and Michael grabs the two ends. He fiddles with the clasp and connects the chain.

"It looks beautiful, Emily!" utters Mrs. Dembitz in admiration.

"Yes, I agree," chimes Mr. Dembitz with a twinkle in his eyes.

Emily shifts to Michael, and he observes the necklace around his wife. Michael's cheeks bulge, seeing the diamonds sparkle by candlelight.

"I requested Pastor Färber to make it for you. I wanted to give you hope, Emily, never to give up, and Pastor Färber agreed with me, stating that we can all use hope," says Michael.

"Thank you, Michael," Emily kisses Michael on his lips.

The next four months pass in what seems like a blink of an eye for the Dembitz and Adelmans; it's April of 1943. Emily is nine months into her pregnancy; for any day or time, her baby will be brought into the world. Since Hanukkah, Emily always wears the necklace Michael gave to her. Unfortunately, things aren't looking too good; Pastor Färber's church donations lessen due to the impact scale of the war. With fewer donations, it's more stressful to afford food for everyone.

Still, everyone makes do with what they have. That evening Pastor Färber visits the secret room and gives everyone more news. When he arrives, Emily is sleeping in her half-sized corridor, and Michael stands nearby. He watches her sleep. Mr. and Mrs. Dembitz are in the secret room and listen to what Pastor Färber says. Michael hears them talking while listening in on the conversation.

"I have a troubling matter that needs to be brought to your attention," mutters Pastor Färber to Mr. and Mrs. Dembitz.

"The other night, while I was preaching my sermon, a group of Nazi soldiers attended church. They were unarmed, of course, and sat within the church, following along with the scripture. Suddenly, one of them rose, and my guess; is he left to use the restroom. The restroom is up in the stairwell and across from my corridors. A couple minutes went by, and the soldier that went upstairs ambled back down and sat next to his other soldier buddies, whispering.

I do not know what they were whispering; I continued with the sermon. After I was done, the church, of course, as you hear from where you are, would praise the Lord by singing hymns. Before the church began to sing, one of the German soldiers nodded and acknowledged what the other soldier had whispered in his ear. After church and with everyone gone, my wife and I talked, and I couldn't help but feel a sudden chill down my spine. I have a terrible feeling in my heart about those soldiers that attended church."

Dead silence fills the atmosphere. Emily's parents' skin turns pale.

"Do you think these Nazi soldiers discovered us? We were all quiet as mice like always during the hours of your church service," shudders Mr. Dembitz.

"Frank, I honestly don't know if they have found out or not, but I felt it was best to bring this to your attention." Pastor Färber frolics with his hands nervously.

Mr. Dembitz bites his lips. They sink into a thin line as he stares at his wife. Mrs. Dembitz has a worried look on her face, her eyes fill with terror, and her lips tug against her teeth.

"I will let you know if anything more happens, but for now, the best thing is to pray to the lord for the best," advises Pastor Färber.

Mr. Dembitz nods his head and agrees with his most valued friend. Pastor Färber exits the secret room, and Mr. Dembitz embraces his wife. They both hold onto each other tightly; they pray and hope together that they haven't been discovered. Michael sits on the floor near his wife, Emily, and prays with all his heart.

That night after Pastor Färber is done with church, he and his wife decide to spend their nights, from now on, in the pastor's corridor. The threat of soldiers storming the church crosses everyone's minds. The pastor and his wife stay alert in case they need to notify everyone in hiding.

It's three in the morning, and everyone is asleep. Michael slumbers on the floor, in the half-sized corridor, and near Emily from praying himself to sleep. Then, out of nowhere, Emily awakens quickly and is startled.

"Michael, Michael! Oh, Michael, please wake up!" she screams at the top of her lungs. Her screaming wakes Michael and everyone else with a frightening scare. Michael bolts to Emily; Mr. and Mrs. Dembitz dart into the half-sized corridor.

"Emily, what's wrong?" asks Michael franticly aloud.

"What's wrong?" he repeats.

Emily snatches Michael's hand; grips it tightly with all her strength.

"It's happening!" she cries. Mrs. Dembitz, out of her reactions, runs towards the secret room's entrance. When she gets there, she sees Pastor Färber and his wife rushing up the stairs.

"My daughter is in labor. Get some blankets, anything, hurry!" shouts Mrs. Dembitz to them both.

"I'll get some blankets downstairs from our donations!" quickly enacts Pastor Färber's wife. She dashes down the stairwell – passes the altar to get the donated sheets.

Emily screeches in pain. Mrs. Dembitz and Pastor Färber dart up to the secret room, through the doorway, and into the half-sized corridor. Mr. Dembitz and Michael stay close to Emily.

"Just breathe; we're here," says her father.

Still holding Emily's hand, Michael repeats, "I'm right here, Emily! I'm right here; we can do this."

Pastor Färber's wife barges in with several blankets, more than she can carry. Mr. Dembitz and Pastor Färber snatch the blankets and lay them out for the baby's arrival.

"All right, Emily... Take easy breaths, and on my count to three, push..." says Pastor Färber keeping an eye on the baby.

Emily shallows her breaths, and Pastor Färber counts down.

"One, two, push!" he shouts. Emily screams in agony and grips Michael's hand with all her strength. Emily's heart pulsates impulsively; her heart rattles and pounds heavily.

In a few moments, Pastor Färber speaks again, "One more time, Emily!" he shouts.

Emily pushes again; tears and sweat stream and dry her skin. The baby cries endlessly. Emily is breathing harshly with her face beet red like she went biking several miles in the hot summer sun.

"Oh, my stars...." mutters Emily's mother in amazement.

Mr. Dembitz can't believe his eyes. He holds onto his wife's hand tightly, and Pastor Färber's wife flashes a heartwarming smile. Pastor Färber cradles the baby in his hands.

"It's a girl Emily…she's so beautiful!" croaks Pastor Färber wrapping the baby up in one of the blankets.

Pastor Färber hands the newborn over to Michael. Michael is overwhelmed. He cradles in his arms his newborn daughter and shows her for Emily to see. The newborn weeps, and Emily strokes her hand upon the baby's forehead. Emily is still catching her breath.

"Oh, Michael!" she shallows.

Emily caresses her daughter's forehead with the brightest smile.

"She needs a name…." adds Michael, still holding the newborn.

Emily ponders for a moment, "Why don't we name her Michael?" suggests Emily.

The baby squirms beneath the blankets and sobs more.

"Uh…." sighs Michael.

His mind daunts as the image of his mother flashes before him.

"How about…Rachel?" He suggests.

"That's a beautiful name!" squeaks Emily.

"That was my mother's name; having a daughter, I'd name her after my mother," says Michael.

"Rachel…." Emily suspires and creases an undeniable smile.

Everyone stares with overwhelming joy at the newborn Rachel brought into the world.

It is a hardship having a baby while hiding in the secret room. Emily guards Rachel close by in her half-sized corridor, and Pastor Färber, in his spare time, builds a handmade cradle that is big enough to fit in the leftover space by Emily's desk. There is enough room for the baby. Food is scarce due to the lack of donations. So, Pastor Färber and his wife use their own pocket money and gather food for everyone. Pastor Färber's wife sneaks out and brings the food with her basket, despite the looming dangers of the war and soldiers.

She fills her basket to the brim, and other times not, but whatever she has, she brings to the old church. Everyone worries that Rachel will cry during church services, but she mostly sleeps during these times.

The months pass on; it's August of 1943. In the morning, everyone in the secret room is up. Mr. Dembitz brushes his wife's hair, and Emily and Michael are in the half-sized corridor. They whisper to Rachel in Emily's arms. Pastor Färber sits in his study and reads over the Bible with his wife.

Suddenly, the calm silence of the church walls abrupts into a loud, violent bang on the church's front doors. Then, not even a second later – another one blares.

"The Gestapo!" shouts Pastor Färber.

He bolts up from his chair, and its legs shift and crash onto the floor.

"Hurry! Go tell the others. I'll stall as much time as possible so everyone can leave out the back!" pleads Pastor Färber to his wife.

His wife kisses him on the cheek and rushes to the stone wall. She pulls out the brick, and the secret passageway opens. Pastor Färber darts down the stairwell and to the altar. When he arrives at the altar, the massive church doors plunge open with several Gestapo officials. They shuffle in with their guns

while several trucks surround the outside. The engines roar.

"What in God's name gives you the right to come barging in with loaded weapons?" rages Pastor Färber with his arms flailing about.

A Nazi Sergeant points his finger at the pastor, "We have several reports that you, Priest, are sheltering Jews in your church!" yowls the Nazi Sergeant.

"I do not! You're wasting your time, Sergeant!" Pastor Färber is firm, steady, and towers tall to protect everyone in hiding.

The Nazi Sergeant loses his patience and grits his teeth. The Sergeant's boots reverberate and pound violently toward Pastor Färber. He unsheathes his pistol and points it at Pastor Färber's head. The Sergeant clicks his gun, ready to fire.

"Tell me where they are, now!" commands the Nazi Sergeant, violently yelling.

Pastor Färber's wife is in the secret room with the Dembitz and Adelman families, ready to escape. Everyone hears what the Nazi Sergeant yells down below them, and then, without notice, a gunshot fires. It grimly echoes within the church's walls. Everyone's heart sinks, fearing the worst; the Gestapo murders Pastor Färber. Baby Rachel begins crying, and everyone hears the Gestapo talking below in their German language.

"Ein Baby, schnell, schnell!" shouts the Nazi sergeant to his men. Rachel's cries echo within the church walls.

"Take her!" yowls Emily as she passes Rachel to Pastor Färber's wife.

Pastor Färber's wife takes Rachel, and despondence fills her eyes at Emily like a deer in headlights. Emily weeps, tears flood her eyes, and she unclasps her necklace, the Star of David. She showers the chain upon Rachel's blanket.

"I want my daughter Rachel to have this…please, keep it safe with her; now go!" shouts Emily.

She nudges Pastor Färber's wife away with Rachel and the necklace Michael gave Emily months ago. Pastor Färber's wife quickly exits the secret room and pads down the stairs leading into the hallway.

She hears the Gestapo rushing up the stairwell near the altar in the hallway. Pastor Färber's wife's mind flashes and recalls her husband's words, *'if anything is to happen, exit through this passage as an escape route. It's the quickest and safest way.'* She pushes in a loose brick, opening another secret passageway. She rushes through, pulls a chain nearby, and the passage behind her shuts.

The Gestapo doesn't see the passage in time, but they discover the stone stairs leading to the secret room where everyone else still stands. The Gestapo barge into the room, and the officials seize everyone. Two soldiers hold down Mr. Dembitz and drag him away while he screams out his daughter's name countless times.

"Emily!"

Another soldier tears away Mrs. Dembitz from Emily. Mrs. Dembitz screams. Her screams trigger Michael's memories of his mother being taken in the same violent manner.

"Mama, Papa!" wails Emily as loud as she can.

One soldier locks Michael by his arms, and the soldier waits until the Sergeant snatches Emily away. With all his strength, the Sergeant grips Emily by her arm, and Michael kicks the soldier holding him. The soldier grunts and Michael pushes him down. With the soldier away, Michael runs at the Sergeant to tackle him. The Sergeant observes Michael coming, tosses Emily aside, and the Nazi Sergeant steps to the side. Emily yelps and teeters on the floor. The Sergeant counters and pins Michael down on the ground. With Michael on the floor, the Sergeant whips Michael with his pistol. He bruises him to the point where he cannot stand.

Blood seeps from Michael's nose and lip. He is too weak to fight back. The soldier Michael pushes away snatches Emily from the ground.

The soldier's fingernails dig beneath her skin. Emily wriggles and squirms, but she can't escape.

The Sergeant clicks his pistol back and aims his gun at Michael, who is on the floor. Emily sobs more at the scene. She is not able to hold back her tears. Michael is defenseless. The Sergeant towers over with his pistol, Michael gazes into the barrel, and his breathing is wild. Time seems to stop for Michael as the Sergeant levels his weapon and taps his finger against the trigger, but the Sergeant stops.

He smirks, "You have guts, Jew, knocking down a Nazi official!" croaks the sergeant.

Rage seethes inside the Sergeant, for he desires to shoot Michael; kill him, but an idea creeps inside his head.

"Though shooting you would be too easy for you, so I'll make sure you make it to the camps alive to suffer!" he hisses vulgarly to Michael.

"Take her away!" commands the Nazi sergeant to the soldier. The soldier obeys and drags Emily away. Michael listens to the sounds of Emily's sobbing; it echoes throughout the church. While the soldier takes her away to the gray trucks, the sergeant grips the back of Michael's neck and drags him out of the church. He throws him like cattle into one of the gray trucks.

Everyone is transported to the Westerbork Transit Camp. At that moment, everyone separates from each other and boards separate trains.

Crowds of over a thousand Jews overfill the transit camp. They deport to the concentration camps they are assigned to. Countless Nazi soldiers sequester everyone away from each other. They herd Jews to board the trains.

Emily loses her parents, but she finds Michael. Michael sees her within the crowds and exerts himself beyond limits to reach his wife, Emily.

"Emily, Emily!" shouts Michael in pain from the beatings he had endured.

The crowds ram into Emily as she bumps into random people.

"Michael, Michael!" she screams aloud to reach him.

Eventually, they reach each other, embrace, and latch on tightly. They use all their strength together to stay together.

Out of nowhere, several Nazi soldiers sever them apart from behind. Michael and Emily try to resist breaking apart.

"No, no!" screeches Michael with anger.

He wails again, "No, no!"

They fight with all their strength together to hold onto each other.

The soldiers are resistant and ruthless; they break them apart with great force. The couple feels their bodies slowly drifting away from each other.

"Michael!" cries Emily. All that is left is them holding each other's hands.

"We'll be together forever, I promise, for better or worse. I love you, Emily!" Michael's eyes glisten; their strength drains.

After Michael's words, the couple's hands release apart, separating from each other.

David Edgar Grinnell

CHAPTER TEN

April 27, 2012

Friday night is here! Luna will pick me up from my apartment any minute now. Work at the National Civil War Museum isn't too bad. My boss Hoggins watches me. He observes how I guide everyone around the museum and engage with them. He is impressed with my knowledge and how I present the history in a somewhat funny but entertaining way. It's not too much, over the top, or a bore for groups of people on the tour.

My shift ended at two this afternoon. When I arrived home, I checked my emails and social media. Still, nothing on the ring, and my advertisements are in vain. I'm wasting money paying for these advertisements to find this Michael Luke Adelman. I'm starting to think that this person doesn't exist.... I can't give up because it belongs to *someone*. It was abandoned at the Holocaust Museum. Next time I go to work, I'll use the museum's printer and create flyers. It will help if I post them around the city. I hear the time tick on my clock on the wall. I bite my lips; I'm a nervous wreck. This will be the first time I will meet Luna's family. I wonder what Luna's family will think of me...I, being a Christian, dating Luna, who is Jewish.

Judging from how Luna is around me, I figure it won't be a big deal because we're dating. My eyes fixate on the clock. It ticks by...it's five minutes before six-thirty, and I glare at the mysterious gold ring belonging to Michael Luke Adelman. I haven't found this man..... There's a knock at my door. I'm frantic; this is it! The ring jostles in my palm from the knocking. I stumble, snatch the box, put the ring back inside, and without thinking, I randomly stuff it in my pocket.

I go over to the door and answer it. I sway my hair back, straighten my shirt, and open the door. It's Luna; she stands there wearing the Star of David with six diamonds on the endpoints of the star she always has around her neck.

"Hey, handsome!" she says vibrantly. She hugs me and kisses me. I kiss her back.

"Ready to go?" she adds with a smile.

"Yes...." I fiddle with my hands and rub them together.

Luna's eyes wander at me, and she caresses my cheek and laughs.

"Don't worry! My family won't bite; you'll love them! It's just going to be my mother, grandmother, you, and me over."

The gleam in her eyes makes me smile.

"I trust you," I say to her while placing my hand on top of hers upon my cheek.

She strokes her thumb against my cheek and stops. I walk into the hall, lock my door, and exit with Luna outside to her car. She gets into her car, starts it up, and I plop myself on the passenger's side. We drive to her mother's house. It takes about twenty minutes from where I lived in DC to arrive.

As Luna drives the car up the driveway, I note that the house is an average size for the suburbs, and from the outside, it looks quaint and inviting.

"This is it...." she says to me.

Luna grips her keys and takes them out of the ignition.

"It's a nice place," I add, looking at the house from the passenger side of the car.

Luna laughs at my comment, "It's doable," she replies as we get out of the car.

Luna and I saunter to the front door that is up the stairs on the porch. There is outdoor furniture on it. Two wicker chairs are near each other, with a wicker-glass table between them. My eyes catch Luna's mother through the front glass door. She observes her daughter and me on the porch. We stand and wait at the front door.

"Hey, come on in!" Luna's mother hobbles awkwardly and lurches towards the front door very strangely. I remember Luna telling me about her mother's movement disease. Luna's mother opens the door as I grab and hold it open for Luna to walk in first.

Luna hugs her mother.

"Hey, mom," she says.

Luna assists her mother walk further into the house so I can enter.

"Mom, I'd like you to meet the special man I've been telling you and grandma about!" says Luna, introducing me.

"Howdy, ma'am. I'm Charlie Campel," I say to her mother while extending my hand for a handshake.

"Awe, nice to meet you! And please, no handshake for you; you get a hug!" she embraces me with a warm, welcoming hug.

I flash a smile when I have my arms around her.

"Thank you, Ms. Braun," I politely say.

"Oh, please! Call me Rachel...." insists Luna's mother.

I nod, and Luna invites me to sit in the parlor.

"Sit down, make yourself at home."

I take my shoes off, and being polite, I set them to the side so they aren't in anyone's way. Then, I sit down at the end of the sofa.

The sofa has four chairs connected, and Luna's mother, Rachel, staggers a bit sideways, and Luna tries to go over to help. It is like her mother is going to trip.

"It's alright, dear," buzzes Rachel to her daughter.

Luna's mother makes it over to the chair and sits down, and Luna takes a seat next to me.

"So, Luna was telling me about how you took a trip through the aisle!" Rachel chuckles with humor in her voice.

I laugh and think about how I fell and knocked the shelves over.

"Yes, we heard it was quite a trip...." says an older lady's voice. I look over and see an old lady slowly crippling to the chair by the mantled fireplace. She sits down as Luna introduces me to her.

"Charlie, I'd like you to meet my grandma, Em," glees Luna.

"It's a pleasure to meet you, ma'am," I add, nodding my head. Luna's grandmother smiles with a sparkle in her eye; she is happy to finally meet me.

"Yes, it's wonderful to finally meet you! Luna has told me a lot about you. She couldn't stop talking about you," teases Luna's grandmother.

"Grandma!" cries Luna to her grandmother.

I notice Luna's face blushing and turning bright pink. I chuckle under my breath, seeing Luna's face blushing.

"What are you laughing at?" she asks with a smile at me.

I just shake my head with a smile because I am happy that she is blushing about me.

"Nothing...." I answer.

I make a flirty, cute face, and everyone laughs at my facial expression. I glare at Luna, and something catches my eye on the mantle by the fireplace. It's a black-and-white photo, but I can't see the image clearly from a distance. Everyone sees me looking at the picture, and Luna's grandmother's eyes pique interest in it because of the look on my face.

Luna's grandmother looks up at the picture.

"That was so long ago; that's my husband and I getting married in a church in Europe."

Luna's grandmother's face turns despondent. Her eyes reflect a cadaverous gloom.

"Your husband?" I inquire with puzzlement because he isn't here in the parlor with us.

"Grandma, you don't have to tell him…." croaks Luna.

"It's alright, sweet pea. It doesn't bother me as much as it used to; it's in the past now. But, young people need to know what happened during that period of history."

Luna's grandmother reclines back into her chair, settling into a deep mentation. Her eyes glitter with a shine, but her lips sink into her mouth. Then, it clicks in my mind what she will start talking about.

"You were in the Holocaust?"

Silence fills the room when I say those words, and finally, Luna's grandmother slowly nods. Her head shifts back up to the wedding picture. Luna's grandmother takes a deep breath.

"Mama, you don't have to if you're not up to it...." Rachel's voice is shallow and muffled.

Luna's grandmother shakes her head, "The man you see in the picture is my husband, Michael Luke Adelman. We grew up together; we spent our young years hiding within the church where we got married."

After Luna's grandmother told me this, my mind races, and my jaw drops, but I pick it back up to conceal my flabbergasted state. I think about the ring from the Holocaust Museum–the one I found on the floor during the tour! My mind is in absolute shock. I grace my hand into my pocket and touch the box where I have Michael's wedding ring.

"May I ask what happened to Michael, your husband?" I ask, zoning in like an eager child.

Luna's grandmother doesn't look at us as she tells her story: "The last time I saw Michael was at the Westerbork Transit Camp, and we became separated within the camp. We were crowded onto different trains and crammed in a small boxcar cab. I don't know how long I was on that train; I was terrified in the crowded space of the train cab. During the ride, several people became ill; most vomited on the train as it clicked along the tracks. Finally, I arrived at Bergen-Belsen with several other Jewish women. We were forced to work hard labor, having barely anything to keep us covered with, and our heads were completely shaved. Later, many began to starve, and I was starved. I saw my own ribcage, and a typhus epidemic arose sometime in March of 1945. It killed over ten thousand prisoners.

I remember waking up in the barracks; many next to me died from the disease. Decaying corpses lay all around me. Worms slithered and feasted upon them. In April of 1945, the camp was finally liberated by British troops. I survived, and one of the soldiers took me and carried me into the trucks. Very few survived the camp, and I remember seeing the troops set fire to the entire center as the trucks took me away. The base was burnt into the ground. The soldiers burnt everything to prevent the further spread of the disease, and I went under intensive medical treatment. I was transferred to London, England–a month after Nazi Germany surrendered.

While in England, I searched for information on my mother, father, and husband, Michael, to see if they had survived. I went to the Red Cross; studied countless lists of names but found nothing. I tried asking around, but nobody had any information, so I stayed in England. I hoped and prayed that I would find them and my daughter Rachel. The months passed on, and finally, the war officially ended. A year later, I returned to the Red Cross to find information on everyone.

I learned that my mother was sent to the Buchenwald Concentration Camp in Germany and that she died from extreme working labor. I began to cry as I heard a small child's voice, "mommy!" I turned around, and it was my daughter, Rachel, who was only four at the time, with Pastor

Färber's wife. I remembered Rachel had on the necklace Michael gave me, and ever since then, she has worn it until Luna was born.

One month after reuniting with my daughter, there was a knock at my flat in England. I answered the door, and it was Ben, Michael's best friend from school. I welcomed him in as he knew I was married to Michael. He told me he met Michael after Michael was transferred from Auschwitz to the Mauthausen concentration camp. My husband stuck with Ben for as long as he could; he told Ben about me and our daughter Rachel.

Ben told me my husband's will and strength were strong. He kept our daughter and me in his mind as motivation. Michael also told Ben that my father had died at Auschwitz in the gas chamber. After that, Ben told me the saddest news I've ever heard.... He informed me that Michael died from a death march, and then Ben took out Michael's ring from his pocket. He gave it to me and placed it in my hand. I wept and clutched the ring into my palm. Then, I fell onto the floor." Luna's grandmother Emily groans a shallow breath.

I observe Luna; she bolts from the sofa next to me, and her face sours into bitter sorrow. She storms out of the parlor, and I go after her a few moments later. I follow her into the kitchen and inquire.

"What's wrong?" A dead gloom hangs over us.

"It's my entire fault! I lost grandpa's ring, and I know how much that ring means to my grandma." she sobs, and her breaths are shallow and broken.

Luna weeps and shrouds her face.

"I feel guilty, ashamed. I lost my grandfather's ring!"

I stand there and wallow at her words.

"Luna...." I putter. Luna looks up at me as I see a tear or two gliding down her cheek.

"I have something to tell you...." I finally add.

My hands grace upon her shoulders. Luna stands there, her eyes squint at me, and her eyebrows sparse apart. I take in a deep breath and reach into my pocket. I take out the box. My eyes glare down at the box for a few seconds. Luna's eyes follow mine. I open the box, and Luna sees Michael Luke Adelman's ring.

She gasps in total shock. Both of her hands shroud her mouth.

"Where did you..." Luna can't finish her question.

"I found it at the Holocaust Museum while on a self-guided tour. I tried searching for the owner of this ring, but everyone I asked in the museum said it wasn't theirs; I did everything I could to find Michael! I posted advertisements online, checked my emails for any leads, and still nothing.... I was even going to create flyers and post them around the city."

Silence fills the room, and the clock in the kitchen ticks. The box is in my hand, and the ring shines from the main kitchen light. Luna takes another look at the ring. Her eyes are wide as she studies it.

"My grandma gave me my grandpa's ring and told me that when I find the one that's right for me, I should give this ring to him. She told me to keep it, take care of it, cherish it, and give it to the man I fall in love with and marry.

So, I held on to it, carrying it with me wherever I went and cherished it close to my heart just like this necklace...." Luna clasps her necklace into her hand and grips it.

"I was supposed to keep it close to me just like I will always keep my future husband close to my heart forever. But that day, when I went to the Holocaust Museum to pay my respects to all who lived and died, I didn't realize I had lost grandpa's ring. I didn't know until I came into the Hall of Remembrance.... I tried all I could to find it; I cried and cried, never forgiving myself because it was my responsibility to treasure it. I felt like I let my grandfather down by losing his wedding ring, but here you had it this whole time. You found it the day I lost it, and I can tell you took excellent care of it!" Luna wipes her tears away.

I smile at her, and my hand caresses her cheek.

"I always took care of this ring because I knew this ring belonged to someone. So now, I know this ring belongs to you, Luna...." I shut the box and gave back Michael's ring to her.

"Charlie…" Luna stares at the box in her hands.

After a few moments with the box in her hands, I set my hand on top of hers. We stand there for a moment, and finally, Luna takes the box with Michael's ring inside.

"I told grandma the first day she came over to my mom's house about me losing grandpa's ring. I told her I let grandpa down and didn't deserve a good man. Because how can I cherish a loving man when I can't take care of the ring my future husband will end up wearing? I could tell my grandmother was a bit upset, but instead of yelling at me, she told me not to worry too much because my grandpa's ring is in a place where millions won't forget. Those millions who visit the museum will always cherish him in their hearts along with the millions who lived and died during the Holocaust."

After Luna's words, we embrace, and I kiss her on her forehead. Luna rests her head against my chest and listens to my heartbeat.

Soon, Luna's grandmother wobbles into the kitchen.

"I'm sorry to interrupt you both, but I'm heading off to bed; it's nine-thirty, and I'm thirty minutes past my bedtime." Luna's grandmother embraces her granddaughter with a kiss on her cheek.

"I should get going," I follow.

"You're more than welcome to stay. Just because I'm going to bed doesn't mean you have to leave," adds Luna's grandmother crippling up to the backstairs.

"No, it's fine. I have work tomorrow morning at seven."

Luna stares at me, "Maybe I can visit you at work sometime," she suggests with a wink.

"I'd love that!" I squeal to Luna with a smile.

She laughs, "Ok, I'll work something out soon!"

She kisses me on the cheek. I kiss her lightly on her lips. She ambles away from me to follow her grandmother, and her eyes radiate with light. I hear her footsteps creak the backstairs, and I make my way back into the parlor to say goodbye to Luna's mother, Rachel.

"Thank you for allowing me to come over," I say to Rachel, who is still sitting on the sofa.

"You're welcome to come back anytime," she smiles brightly at me.

I bend down and hug her, "I will!"

Rachel hugs me back with a smile, "You make my daughter Luna the happiest she's ever been, and I can't thank you enough for making her feel special. I feel so bad that my daughter takes care of me more than she does to take care of herself. I try my hardest to stand and walk on my own, so Luna doesn't have to take care of me. I miss being independent, and it's not fair to my daughter," says Rachel.

I nod, "Luna is very special to me. I've never met anyone like her. She makes me feel special, and I love every moment I spend with her."

Rachel gives me a bright smile from what I've said about her daughter Luna.

"Enjoy every moment you have with her. She deserves a good man to whom she can always give her heart to."

My heart aches at Rachel's words about her daughter and her hopes for our relationship. I bend down, grab my shoes, and tie them. I'm at the front, ready to leave as I turn around.

"I will always give my heart to her for better or worse." I give Rachel a promise.

I exit the house, walk out further, and find a night taxi back home to my apartment.

CHAPTER ELEVEN

Saturday passes, and on Sunday, my phone rings.

"Hello?" I answer.

It's Luna's delicate voice.

"Hey Charlie, I have some news. It's my grandmother...she passed away earlier on Saturday night or Sunday morning. She went to bed Saturday night at her normal time like she always does, and the next morning, she didn't wake up."

Luna's breath shallows. From the tone of her voice, I sense she is trying to be strong about her grandmother's death.

"I'll be there. When's the funeral?" I mutter to her.

"It will be tomorrow, Monday, at the Tifereth Israel Congregation Synagogue in DC. It's at four in the afternoon," she solemnly states after a brief silence.

More silence drowns across our phones.

I putter, "I'll be there. I'll take a taxi and meet you there."

The phone crackles with static.

"Okay...." answers Luna hanging up the phone.

The moment I hang up, a desire to stop by Luna's and be there for her fuels my being. Yet, I think it the best for her to spend time with her mother. So, I call my boss, Hoggins, and ask him if I could have Monday off and inform him about the funeral. He grants my request and comforts me by saying he'll take care of my shift.

Monday creeps up, and I dress in a coat and tie. It's a black blazer with a light blue lined dress shirt. I slowly knot my dress tie in a trance. The tie is light blue with gold stripes slanting downward.

My eyes shift, it's three in the afternoon, and I amble into the city of DC to catch a taxi.

Eventually, I get into a taxi. I inform the driver to drive to the Tifereth Israel Congregation. *Too bad it's not the taxi driver I had that one day trying to get to my job interview on time. I miss him. Eh, then again... I'm glad it's not the same driver at the same time.*

The driver drops me off at the synagogue. I observe other cars parked within the parking lot. I don't see Luna or her mother, but Luna's car is in the parking lot. So, I go into the sanctuary to meet up with them.

The funeral is sparse. There aren't many people when I wander inside. My eyes catch the closed casket of Luna's grandmother and a small table with the picture of her and Michael next to the casket.

Soon, I see Luna sitting next to her mother in the front row across from the casket. Luna is holding her mother's hand. She is wearing the black dress that she wore on our first date. I observe her facing her mother; she whispers to her, and my eyes catch Luna's Star of David necklace glittering within the temple's light. I rethink the necklace's history and how it was passed down. Rachel also wears a black dress; she stares down at the floor after Luna whispers to her. Rachel mourns and leans onto her other hand with her cane. I wander down and sit in the pew behind them. When I sit down, Luna notices me. She twists her head around to look at me.

She gives me her hand, and I grip it. She squeezes my hand, and I kiss her hand before letting go. Soon, Rachel sees me and turns around to face me. With tears in her eyes, she flashes me a small smile to say hello. I nod my head back with a smile and acknowledge her. There are a few other people in attendance that probably know Luna's grandmother, but I do not know for sure who they are. The funeral service within the synagogue doesn't last long. It's about fifteen or twenty minutes. After the service, the rabbi and a few other temple men carry the casket to the hearse for burial.

We follow the hearse with Luna's car going to the gravesite. I stand next to Luna on her left side. I hold her hand while Luna holds onto her mother's hand from her right. Together, we watch the undertakers gently and delicately lower the casket into the six-foot grave. As it's lowered,

Luna weeps, unable to stay strong. She squeezes my hand tightly. Luna and Rachel trudge to say their last goodbyes when the casket is in the grave.

They both still hold each other's hands. Then, while walking awkwardly with her cane, Rachel stares down at the casket, followed by Luna a few moments later.

Suddenly, Luna releases her mother's hand, drops to her knees, and sobs out loud. She grips the Jewish star that is around her neck. She bows her head down and clutches the necklace like a part of herself has died. Rachel rests her hand on her daughter's shoulder as she cries.

Nobody says anything to each other during or after the funeral. Luna drives back to the house, and I go with them to spend some time. We all sit in the parlor in silence until Luna's mother, Rachel, cripples up from the sofa with her cane.

"Mama?" jolts Luna, like she was awakening from a deathlike trance.

Her eyes follow her mother, and her lips sink.

"I'm going to bed, darling...I just need some time." Rachel staggers toward the stairs.

"I can take you upstairs," suggests Luna to her mother,

"No, dear, I'll be fine," retorts her mother.

Luna rises and stumps over to hug her mother for a few moments.

"I love you, mom," she says softly.

"I love you, too," Rachel kisses her daughter's forehead.

After Rachel kisses Luna, she shuffles awkwardly with her cane upstairs. Luna's eyes watch her mother intently. Luna freezes and stares at the ceiling to make sure Rachel won't fall down the stairs. I hear Rachel's footsteps one at a time and finally on the second floor. The bedroom door shuts quietly.

Luna and I sit together on the sofa in silence. I wrap my arm around her. She cries again from my touch, her body falters, and she lies close to me for comfort. I adjust, lie with her, and snuggle. I hold her in my arms and run my fingers through her dark hair.

"Do you remember the night you came over and afterward when I went upstairs with my grandmother?" asks Luna.

My fingers continue to grace through her hair, and she nuzzles against my chest.

"Yes, I remember. What about it?" I ask as I kiss the top of her head. Luna reflects for a moment.

"That night, when I was upstairs helping grandma to bed, I showed her grandpa's ring and told her that you found it the day I lost it. I told her how well you took care of it and tried to find the person it belonged to."

I bat my eyes and smudge my lips.

"What did she say?" I ask in curiosity.

"She asked me why I didn't let you keep grandpa's ring. Grandma told me that the way you looked at me when we all sat in the parlor was how my grandpa used to look at her. She told me she could sense that you'd do anything for me, always be there for me. Just like how grandpa was there for her."

Luna pauses.

"To be honest, Charlie, I'm afraid…. I'm afraid to fall in love because I don't want to be abandoned, just like my mother was with my father. Seeing what my mother went through was horrible." Luna buries her head into my chest and nuzzles.

My head gently leans down upon the back of hers, inhaling her scent.

"I will always give my heart to you, Luna, for better or worse. All I ask in return is for you to do the same for me, and I will always cherish you, just like I've always cherished your grandfather's ring." I whisper to her.

My hand graces and delicately grips her hand. Luna rolls over to face me.

"I will always cherish you, Charlie. I've never met anyone like you before. You've never judged me, you've never judged me for taking care of my mother like most men I've met, and you've never judged me for my religion."

Luna's eyes gaze into my eyes. A soft wave of light breathes life into them. Her brown eyes gleam with a beauty I cannot describe, but I sense she is afraid by how she looks at me. Her eyes tremble, and the desire to caress her cheek overwhelms my soul.

"I trust in you, Luna. I'll always stand by you for better or worse; I promise," I emphasize and stroke her cheek.

Luna touches my hand that is on her cheek. She closes her eyes and nuzzles her cheek against my hand. At the same time, I feel the gentle grip of her hand touching mine as she opens her eyes to me.

"I love you, Charlie," she softly whispers.

My heart aches at her words. Nobody has ever told me they love me. I shallow the words.

"I love you too, Luna."

We kiss, and I find myself in a trance, lost in the moment. Kiss after kiss, we stare, and Luna reaches over to the coffee table to grab her purse.

She takes out a box and presents her grandfather's ring.

"I want you to have this," she says and slides the ring onto my ring finger.

"Luna...." I shallow. "Are you sure?"

She grips my hand; I feel the ring crushing against my skin and hers.

"Yes, you're the man of my life. I love you with all my heart, Charlie Parker Campel."

We cuddle up together and slowly drift off to sleep.

116

CHAPTER TWELVE

Luna isn't next to me when I wake up. When I sit up on the sofa, my head pounds from oversleeping. I glare at the time clock on the mantel.

"Great Scott," I mutter to myself.

"It's early morning, and I have thirty minutes until my shift at work starts!"

I bolt up and realize that nobody is around; it's quiet. So I stand there until my eyes catch a note Luna left me on the coffee table in front of the sofa.

Hey Charlie,

Mom and I went out to order grandma's tombstone. They will replace the marker on her grave. I left some money for you on the kitchen counter. Take a taxi to work. I'll come by today!

I love you and see you soon.

Love,

Luna

I drop the note down on the coffee table.

"She *really* loves me!" I say, shoving my hands upon my head in disbelief.

I feel something metallic when my fingers grip my head. I study my finger; It's the ring…I smile brightly like a weight is lifting off my shoulders. I cannot get the smile off my face, and I stride to the kitchen. I observe the money Luna left for me. The energy within me consumes my inner being. I have never been so alive! I am vibrant when I depart the house and stride toward the inner city of DC. I catch a taxi to work.

While doing so, I do a little skip and a jump of glee in the air. Then, I laugh to myself, and my emotions are overwhelmed with joy.

"I just want to go to work and get my shift over with, so I can be with Luna!" I squeal.

I notice I am still wearing my funeral clothes, but I don't have enough time to go and change at home.

Finally, I made it to the inner city of DC. I glare at my watch; I have twenty minutes left until my shift begins. I raise my hand to hail a taxi.

"Taxi, taxi!" I shout.

All the city traffic zooms by on the busy streets. Soon, a taxi stops on the side of the road where I stand on the sidewalk. I plop in the back and ask the driver to drive to the National Civil War Museum.

"Ok, you go it," answers the driver.

He nods his head and drives off. While he is driving, rain lightly taps against the roof.

Minutes later, it rains arduously, and I study my watch. The time displays I have ten more minutes until my shift. Eventually, I see the museum in the distance, and my mind eases. I will make it on time.

The taxi driver drives into the parking lot and stops the car.

"Alright, that's forty dollars." The driver glares back at me for the money.

I study the payment meter on the dashboard; it's forty dollars.

"Here you are, sir," I say to him.

I hand him the money Luna left me.

"Thanks a lot. Do you need me to come back to pick you up?" asks the taxi driver.

"No, I'll be fine. Thanks," I add and get out, slamming the door.

After the door shuts, the driver rolls down his window.

"Have a great day, sir," he says politely.

He slightly pulls down his driver's cap to say goodbye to me.

"Good day to you," I answer as I walk up to the main entrance.

I saunter into the museum; I prepare for my shift to begin. When the time is closer, I clock in to start my day. I take a group of tourists that are from a public school and guide them around the museum. I lecture on the history of the exhibits around. I spend most of my shift with all the groups of school tourists on their field trips. Soon, it becomes a quarter to two in the afternoon. I'm near the reception desk and in front of the desk is the main entrance just a few feet away.

My eye catches someone strolling in. It's Luna!

She arrives just like she said she would. The Jewish star she always wears around her neck glitters from the light as she sashays a bit further. She is near the front reception desk and sees me. I stare at her, smile, and lose myself in her eyes. She flashes a smile when she sees me. The warmest light wave radiates within my soul, seeing her before me.

Suddenly, a loud bang, like the sound of a gunshot. Luna falls to her knees, and another gunshot reverberates. I watch her body jolt from the impact, and her body falls sideways to the floor. I look up seeing a skinhead man with a handgun in his hand. He turns around and darts away.

When he turns, I observe a tattoo of the Nazi sigma on the back of his neck. I rush up to Luna, and her blood gushes from her body to the floor. I kneel slowly in total shock. I sob and caress her in my arms. The blood on her body covers my hands.... I bury my head down and cry. Luna is gone. The light within her deep brown eyes fades.

The shooting within the museum is on the news. It's now a crime scene. The police interview several of the witnesses, as am I. Everyone describes the shooter as a skinhead with holes in his blue jeans, wearing a leather jacket, and appearing to be in his early thirties.

I tell the police that the man has a Nazi sigma tattooed on the back of his neck. The police took my eyewitness report and dismissed me to go back home and take it easy, as they would contact me if they needed more questioning.

I take another taxi with tears in my eyes and go back to Rachel's house to tell her the heartbreaking news. Minutes pass, and I arrive at the home just as a police car leaves. I amble into the house, going through the front door, and see Luna's mother on the floor crying. She is holding her own body and sobbing a river of tears. Water fills my eyes as I kneel to her. Rachel looks up at me, and we embrace. Her body falters heavily into mine, for the one we love most is gone.

In the weeks that pass after the day of the shooting, I check in with Rachel at her house. Every day: she would lie in her bed and weep in the darkness of her room. She would cry herself to sleep. While in her grief, I would do chores such as cleaning, sweeping, mopping, and dusting. In the silence of the house, Rachel would weep in pain with a broken heart trying to stay strong.

Rachel and I go to the Tifereth Israel Congregation Synagogue for Luna's funeral. I stay by Rachel the whole time; the necklace Luna always wore is with her inside the casket. It rests around her neck. The funeral is an open casket, and Rachel and I see Luna lying peacefully. Rachel staggers up and cripples along to her daughter's casket with her cane.

She kneels on the step and whispers a prayer to say her goodbyes. I shuffle up behind Rachel when she rises awkwardly. Rachel mooches by me and sits in the front row as I stare at Luna's casket. I kneel slowly on the step, saying my last goodbye.

"You changed my whole life around, Luna. I came to DC to move out from Kentucky, and since I came here, I have gone through nothing but bad luck. That's until my bad luck led me straight to you. You took my soul out that night up on the deck of the dinner cruise. Our love might be over, but I promise you it won't stop there. I will always be here for you. You touched my heart like no one else. So, as you move on from this world, remember me, remember us, and all that we are and were. I love you. I swear to always be true for better or worse. But, Luna, I don't know how I will live without you. I just can't...I can't...." I sob, catching a glimpse of Michael's ring on my ring finger where Luna placed it.

"You have been the one for me," I say, taking off the ring from my finger. Then, with the ring in my hand, I touch Luna's cold hand and slide her grandfather's ring onto her ring finger. My hand clasps around hers for a moment.

"Goodbye, Luna Braun...I will always love you."

Luna is buried next to her grandmother, Emily, in the cemetery as Rachel and I stand. We watch Luna's casket lowering into the ground. The moment her casket rests six feet in the earth, I am hollow.

One morning I switch on the news, and the news reporters have an update on the shooting. The police discovered the shooter and identified him as Travis Hughes, and he had a getaway driver with him. They flash a photo of both the shooter and the getaway driver, and I recognize the getaway driver. He's the taxi driver that took me to work that day of the shooting. His name was Anthony. He is Travis' brother. The motive of the shooting remains unidentified, but there is going to be a trial held within the next couple of weeks.

Rachel was with me when I turned on the news, and later that afternoon, we received a notice in the mail that required us to show up in court for the shooting. Within a few weeks, the court day finally arrives. Rachel and I take a bus to the courthouse. I assist Rachel with getting on the bus, and we sit together, arriving on time. The bus drops us off at the bus stop from the corner where the courthouse stands. I escort Rachel to the courthouse, open the doors for her, and we stagger in.

Soon, more people arrive, and the time for trial approaches. Nobody understands why the shooting happened, so they first placed Rachel on the stand to talk about Luna as a person and to comprehend some idea of why this happened. The police officer of the court escorts Rachel to the stand, and she swears to tell the truth and only the truth. Next, both lawyers ask Rachel personal questions about Luna:

"Ms. Braun, did your daughter have any association or relationship with either man Travis or Anthony Hughes?" asks the attorney.

"No," replies Rachel on the stand.

"Did your daughter Luna ever mention anything to you regarding the Hughes brothers?" asks the attorney glaring at Rachel.

"No, Luna never mentioned anything," she adds.

The attorney reflects for a moment to think of another question.

"What is your daughter's usual routine?" he inquires.

Rachel shallows a deep breath.

"My daughter, Luna, takes care of me most of her day at home, she volunteers at the Tifereth Israel Congregation Synagogue in DC, and she works a full-time job as one of the librarians at the District of Columbia Public Library," answers Rachel.

"What time does she normally go to work at the library?" follows the attorney.

"She works mornings from six-thirty to twelve-thirty during the week and on Saturday, from eight in the morning until eleven in the morning, but she's off on Sundays."

After Rachel's response, the attorney bites his lips and purses them:

"When does she go volunteer at the temple?"

Rachel clears her throat to answer.

"She volunteers during the weekend nights starting at six in the evening."

The attorney quickly asks a follow-up.

"And when does she return home from volunteering at the synagogue, Ms. Braun?"

Rachel does not falter her words.

"She comes home at eight-thirty."

The attorney nods as he paces back and forth across the court.

"How would you describe your daughter, Luna, as a person?" questions the attorney with his final question.

"My daughter is a very kind, sweet, gentle, beautiful woman. She loves her family; she has always taken care of her grandmother and me when she comes to visit. She's passionate and sensitive, always placing the ones she loves first," says Rachel, finishing.

The attorney nods his head again.

"Thank you, Ms. Braun. You may step down," interjects the judge.

"Next to the stand is Charlie Parker Campel. May you please take the stand, Mr. Campel?" requests the judge studying the police reports.

I stand up, walk towards the stand, and a police officer of the court escorts Rachel to her seat. I am at the stand, swear in and sit down.

"Charlie Parker Campel, what is your relationship with Luna Braun, the victim?" asks the attorney.

"She's my girlfriend," I answer back.

"When did you meet Luna Braun, Mr. Campel?" follows the attorney.

"I met her at the grocery store in DC when I crashed into the store shelves. I was trying to help an employee pick up the canned goods he dropped."

The attorney strokes his chin.

"When did you and Luna Braun start dating?" he asks.

"Luna and I started dating about a month and a half ago when she took me on a dinner cruise along the Potomac River."

The attorney nods his head at my answer.

"During your time dating her, Mr. Campel, you got a job working at the National Civil War Museum as a tour guide? The same location where the victim Luna Braun was shot and killed by defendant Travis Hughes?"

The attorney paces back and forth.

"Yes, sir, that is correct!" I say firmly to him.

"What are your work hours, Mr. Campel?" he asks.

"My work hours are from seven in the morning until two in the afternoon."

The attorney jams his fists into his pockets.

"Why did Luna Braun show up to the museum at a quarter to two in the afternoon on the day of the shooting?" he follows.

"The day before the shooting was Luna's grandmother's funeral, and I spent the evening over at Rachel's house with her.

Rachel went upstairs to bed, upset about her mother's death, while Luna and I stayed downstairs in the parlor talking. We told each other that we loved each other more than anything and cuddled, falling asleep. When I awoke, Luna and her mother weren't at the house. Instead, Luna left me a note saying that she and her mother went out to order her grandmother's tombstone. Luna told me she would stop by my work when my shift was almost over, and she left me some money on the counter so I could take a taxi to work."

The attorney's dress shoes scuffle against the hard floors.

"During your time dating Luna Braun, Mr. Campel, did she ever mention anything about the Hughes brothers?" asks the attorney.

"No, Luna never mentioned anything about them," I reply as he continues to pace back and forth.

"Did you, Mr. Campel, see any of the Hughes brothers on the day of the shooting?" asks the attorney with his voice echoing within the courtroom.

"Yes, I did," I explain as his eyes meet mine while he paces towards me.

"Whom did you see?" asks the attorney.

"I saw the getaway driver, Anthony Hughes. He was the taxi driver driving me to work that day." I answer as the attorney drifts away.

"Did you know it was Anthony at the time?" he adds.

"No, I did not know at the time," I say as I study Anthony sitting next to his brother, Travis.

They both wear bright orange jail attire with blank stares like nobody is home.

"Did you see Travis, the shooter, before the shooting occurred?"

The attorney stops and stares at me.

"No, I did not see Travis Hughes before the shooting. But I saw him when he pulled the trigger inside the museum," I say, never leaving my gaze upon his.

The attorney nods his head having nothing else to ask me.

"Ok, Mr. Campel, you may step down," adds the judge.

The judge clears his throat.

"Defendant Travis Hughes, please take the stand!" demands the judge loud and clear. Everyone is silent. The shackles on Travis reverberate as he lurches to the stand.

He has a dark demeanor about him, a cold presence lurking within him. With his back turned to me, my eyes catch his Nazi sigma tattoo on the back of his neck.

"Do you swear to tell the truth, nothing but the truth, so help you God?" asks the officer.,

"I do," says Travis chillingly.

"You may take a seat," advises the officer.

The officer walks to the side. The attorney rises and starts asking questions.

"Did you, Travis Hughes, have any relations with Luna Braun, the victim?" asks the attorney.

Travis stares blankly for a moment; his eyes are bleak and hollow.

"No," he lowly mutters.

"Did you see the victim any time before the shooting?" asks the attorney.

"Yes," replies Travis swiftly.

"When and where did you see Luna Braun before the shooting?" asks the attorney to him.

Travis molds out a grin.

"I saw her one-night walking into the Godforsaken Jewish temple on 7701 16th Street. I was smoking a cigarette by my car parked on the other side of the street. She was wearing the stupid Jewish star around her neck!"

He leans back to adjust his posture.

"What did you do when you saw her?" asks the attorney.

"I quickly got my brother, who was in my car. I pointed the heathen out to him. We had a few laughs and cracked Jewish jokes," answers Travis with a laugh and licking his lips.

I ball my hand into a fist as rage swells within me.

"How and why did you devise the plan for the shooting since the day you saw her?" asks the attorney.

Travis smiles with a slight chuckle.

"A beautiful Jewish broad like that doesn't deserve to walk on this earth. I am doing God's work and eliminating Jews for the Aryan race. The voice of God told me to kill her.

So, my brother followed her home, we found out where she goes daily, and one day we saw the Jewish heathen pulling into her driveway with that man and the Jewish harlot's mother." Travis's finger points at Rachel and me. He continues.

"My brother and I decided on that day we saw them that we would shoot the infidel with the star the following day. The next day, the day of the shooting, my brother and I were in his taxicab. My brother had to work his shift, so he dropped me off at the house. I saw her and the mother driving off somewhere.

After that, I waited for them. I stalked their neighborhood, hidden and unseen. When they arrived back, I was going to go in for the kill until my brother called me on my phone. He told me he picked up that man earlier!" He says, pointing at me.

"My brother drove him to the National Civil War Museum. I told my brother I was going to kill the Jewish harlot right there and then. My brother told me no because I would need a fast getaway. By then, I saw her driving off again, and I told my brother she was heading off to work.

My brother picked me up at twelve-thirty in the afternoon when his shift was done. So, I walked to the public library. I waited around for him to show up. At twelve-thirty, I got a call from my brother. He told me he was almost at the library. At the same time, I saw the Jew leave. I stalked her far behind. I saw her get in her car, start it, and drive up the driveway of the parking lot. My brother was a few seconds late picking me up with his taxicab. We caught up to her car and followed her to the National Civil War Museum."

Travis bites his lips proudly, and after a few moments, he takes a deep breath of relief.

"And that's when I killed the pheasant, Jew!"

Everyone in the courtroom is silent. Nobody says anything, and trust me, if I dropped a pin, everyone would hear it. Everyone is flabbergasted by Travis' story of why he murdered Luna. He did it because she was Jewish, and everyone knew it from his story. He is insane, along with his brother! I want to lash out at Travis and beat him to a bloody pulp, but I know that isn't the answer.

Finally, the judge speaks.

"You may...step...down," he mutters in absolute shock.

Travis steps down, and everyone in the room hears his shackles clank as he shuffles, and he grins a sinister, evil smile.

"I believe there is no need for other witnesses on the stand," adds the judge.

The courthouse is adjourned for a break while the jury decides the skinheads' fate. A few hours dwindle as all in the courtroom sit in dreadful silence.

"Everyone, please rise," the judge requests and breaks the silence.

"Jury of the court, how do you find the defendant?"

"Guilty," announces the jury without questioning or regretting their ruling.

The judge nods his head.

"I hereby rule the defendants, Anthony Hughes and Travis Hughes, guilty of the murder of Luna Braun. Both will serve solitude in different cells away from each other for life in a psychological ward prison to never see the light of day; court adjourned!" pronounces the judge laying his gavel to rest.

I am happy with the judge's decision. They should suffer for what they have done, I think to myself as I watch Anthony and Travis being escorted out of the courthouse by several police officers.

After they depart, I go over to Luna's mother, Rachel, and hug her. She embraces me back. I escort Rachel as she strolls along with her cane and hobbles awkwardly like she always does. She and I get a taxicab outside the courthouse and ride back to her house. It is the evening when we arrive home. I fix Luna's mother's dinner, sit with her at the table, and eat. We do not say anything to each other, but we like our company.

After eating, we clean the dishes, and she washes them while I dry and put them away.

When we finish, Rachel speaks to me.

"I'm off to bed…it's been a long day," she mutters.

I nod my head and agree.

"Would you like me to escort you upstairs?" I gesture.

"No, thanks. I need to do this on my own," she retorts.

She shuffles awkwardly to a door that's in the kitchen. She opens the door and shifts to me.

"You may stay the night if you'd like. There is a guest room that is always available for you," she told me.

"I'd love to. It *has* been a long day," I reply.

Rachel turns to face the door with stairs leading to the second floor.

With her cane in hand, she walks up to the second floor. Moments later, I hear her bedroom door closing afterward. I do not stay up too long myself, and I shuffle upstairs.

I wander past Luna's bedroom. I stare in by the doorway. The room is dark and empty.

After a few moments, I enter the guest room next door to her room. I lie on the guest bed and drift off to sleep as I think about Luna, and begin to dream.

Light-waves they are. I stare to see a group of people bathed in the light. It isn't clear to me who the group is. Suddenly, I hear a familiar voice echoing softly to me.

"Don't worry about me...I am in a better place now but never forget...." says the voice.

The image ripples become clearer, and I see Emily, Michael, and their parents together. A figure looms in front of them as their image embers into focus like a streamline of tealight candles. It's Luna with her final words.

"Never forget them...."

David Grinnell who also goes by the pen name David Edgar Grinnell is a poet, author, and scholar from Cleveland, Ohio. He was born 1992 in Norfolk, Virginia, but grew up in the suburb of Bedford. While drawing inspiration from vulnerability, Grinnell writes a diverse range of works which includes historical fiction, romance, gothic, and more. He has his bachelor's degree in English and is currently studying for his M.A. in English. Besides writing and academics, Grinnell is a songwriter, guitarist, and is in a Cleveland band called Naissance.

Other Titles by David Edgar Grinnell

Ashes — Alice Reaper departs from her hometown Boydton, Virginia after her father's tragic death. She begins anew in the small town of Bedford, Ohio as nightmares and the memories of the past haunt her. Longing for inner-peace, she struggles against her own darkness, demons, and the ashes of the life she once lived.

Moonglade — Love, longing, heartache, and loneliness are illuminated in this heartfelt collection from David Edgar Grinnell. Building on themes of budding relationships, misunderstood feelings, and innocent first loves, *Moonglade* creates a narrative that is relatable to everyone looking for love and companionship. Immerse yourself in a world of gothic romantic poetry that shines a soft light on finding and losing love in the twenty-first century.

What Others are Saying About Lightwaves

"I was pleased with the care David took in telling a Jewish-centered story. *Lightwaves* marries the past and present together, two stories converging into one. It plays on hope and darkness and, ultimately, the danger Jews have faced throughout the centuries into our modern era just for being Jewish. Having read the author's published work, I think this is one of his best pieces. I read the entire novella curled up on a cold afternoon, ignoring my puppy and forcing her to cuddle with me as I couldn't put it down.

It's tragic, yet filled with light, twists, and turns with big moments that surprised me. It is where the author shines. He did that beautifully in his novel *Ashes* as well. For me, this story hit home in 2022 with the rise of antisemitism worldwide. We need more stories that tell the Jewish experience today. Yes, this story has a Holocaust backdrop, but ultimately it is set in today's world and shows that something as small as wearing a Magen David (the Jewish star) today is just as dangerous as it's ever been.

Lightwaves isn't just a Jewish story as the protagonist isn't Jewish, but southern a boy from Kentucky. It's a story of love, finding your people and the safety in them, familial connections, and the history that ties us all together. The flashbacks are reminiscent of Anne Frank's Diary and what the Frank family and so many others went through during the war, relying on the kindness of neighbors and risking their own lives to save a friend. I enjoyed the way David wrote this book, and even though it's not a long book, it covers so much in a nuanced and careful manner. I was happy with the representation given in this story and think many will enjoy it."

—Adanna Moriarty, Bestselling Author, *Threadbare: A Patchwork of Poems that Make a Life*

"Flashing back and forth in time, Lightwaves captures the beauty and tragedy of one of the most horrific happenings of our times, the Holocaust. Weaving webs of connections, and their consequences throughout the years, Grinnell manifests how both love and hate have far-reaching effects. Filled with heart-wrenching moments as well as silly sweetness, Lightwaves is a lovely novella that adds to the literary traditions around World War Two and the Holocaust."

—Enoch Black